On the stage, a man was sitting writing at a desk. He had dark brown curly hair and wore a collarless shirt and gray trousers. Debbie squeezed my elbow. "That's him!" she said.

I figured it must be.

The music grew softer and a train whistle blew and Joe Brady began talking. I don't know what came over me, but I felt like bursting into tears. I didn't know if it was Joe Brady that was killing me or the poetry he was saying, but it was as if I was swept away hearing him go on like that.

When he finished talking, he kept writing, and the other actors and actresses began to speak, but I didn't pay attention to what they were saying. I couldn't take my eyes off Joe Brady.

Best Wishes, Joe Brady

BY
MARY
POPE
OSBORNE

Joe Brady

Random House Sprinters

Random House · New York

For my twin, Bill Pope

*I would like to thank Bill Osborne, Marjorie Osborne,
and Minnie Osborne for the inspiration they have given me.*

*I am grateful also to Meredith Mullins and Jean Marzollo
for their helpful suggestions; and to my editor,
Amy Ehrlich, for her invaluable guidance and support.*

Best Wishes,
Joe Brady

1

The first time I heard Joe Brady's name was on Ida Faye's front porch. It was a Sunday afternoon in June about a week after I'd graduated from high school, and I'd gone up the street to Ida Faye's, figuring one hot place to sit was about as good as another. "Hey, Sunny," Ida Faye said when she saw me crossing her yard.

"Hey." I climbed the steps and plopped down in the chair next to Ida Faye. Parts of the Sunday paper were spread in her lap and all over the floor.

"Hot," she said, fanning herself with the funnies.

"You're not kidding. How come you're not cooking? I thought sure I'd find you cooking." Ida Faye almost always cooked a huge—and I mean *huge*—meal for all her relatives every Sunday. She was eighty-seven years old, but she had a lot more spirit than most people half her age.

"None of the family could come today," she said.

"Oh. Where's Ray?" Ray was Ida Faye's grandson; he was the only relative who actually lived with her.

"Ray's there—right over yonder . . ."

Sure enough, under the pine trees amongst a bunch of car parts and old tires, the bottom half of Ray Perkins's body was sticking out from under the hood of the red Chevette he was working on. Working on cars was what Ray did for a living those days. "I'm going to go bother him for a second," I said. I got up from my chair and headed over to Ray. I slapped him on the rear end and said, "Hey, silly!"

Ray looked up and wiped his face. "Hey, Sunny."

"Where were you last night?" I said.

"I guess I was out."

"I guess you were—I came here looking for you."

Ray smiled, and he went back to working under the hood of the car. I stood near him for a minute or two, then headed on back to Ida Faye.

"Did you see this?" she said, picking a piece of the newspaper off the floor.

"What is it?"

She found what it was she wanted. "Here." It was a picture of a man and a woman hugging.

"Who're they?" I said.

"That fellow there's Joe Brady."

"Who's he?"

"You don't know? You must not follow that story."

"What story?"

"*Another Love.*"

"No, no, I cut back on all my soaps. I was getting too hooked."

"Well, he's that boy who got killed by the mob last spring—he was mine and Debbie's favorite. He's going to be in this play in Summerville."

"Great." I watched Ray straighten up and slam down the hood of the car. He lit a Pall Mall and started over to the house.

"Going to sit with us awhile?" Ida Faye asked him as he climbed the steps.

"No ma'am, getting me a beer." Ray opened the screen door and went inside.

"Oh, I wish he wouldn't start drinking that beer so early," Ida Faye said.

"I guess it's better than some other things," I said in a low voice.

"I reckon," she said. We understood each other perfectly. We never came right out and talked about the drug problem Ray used to have. That was when he sang and played guitar with a country western band. He lived outside Charlotte back then.

A moment later Ray came back out carrying his beer. His bony face still had a little car grease on it, and his straight brown hair was brushed back wet behind his ears.

He winked at me, then headed on down the steps. "Where you going?" I said.

"Out for a while."

I wanted to say take me with you, but I didn't. I mean, I was forward with men, but I was also smart. I wasn't going to embarrass myself to death by having Ray say no. I watched him get into his station wagon. "Have fun," I said half sarcastically.

Ray raised his hand in farewell, then backed the car out into the street.

Boy, this was just the kind of thing that could burn me up. Ever since Ray Perkins had moved back home last year, he'd acted like I was still too young to go on dates or anything with him. He was only six years older than me. That's a right big difference when you're both children, but we were grown now—I'd just turned eighteen, and I didn't think the age difference should matter so much anymore. But I guess that's one of the dangers when you've known someone your whole life—they get a picture of you fixed in their heads and it's hard to pry it loose from them.

"Where's he going?" I asked Ida Faye as we watched Ray drive off.

"Who knows?" she said.

I stared down the road.

"The play's called *Look Homeward, Angel*," she said. "Isn't that a pretty name?"

"What play?" I'd forgotten what we'd been talking about.

"The one that Joe Brady's in—that soap opera star. It's at the dinner theater at the mall."

"Oh yeah."

"Edna Shivers saw *Shenandoah* there. She thought it was the best thing she'd ever seen."

"Well, I'd like to go there sometime," I said.

"They serve liquor, honey. I think you have to be eighteen."

"Well, I am eighteen now! Can't anyone around here get that straight?"

Ida Faye just smiled at me. "Well, if I can get Debbie and Boyd to take me, we'll give you a call."

"Please do," I said.

The second time I heard Joe Brady's name was when Debbie called me a week later. Debbie was married to Ray's younger brother, Boyd Perkins; they lived next door to Ray and Ida Faye. "Hey, Sunny," she said when I picked up the phone. "You want to go to the dinner theater on Tuesday to see Joe Brady?"

"I think I do. How much does it cost?"

"Twenty dollars per person."

"Twenty dollars per person?"

"They serve food there, you know," Debbie said.

"Well, what in the world do they serve? Steaks and lobsters?"

"I don't know, Sunny."

"Well, do we have to eat? Can't we just watch the show?"

"No, Sunny. Make up your mind and call me back."

"Oh, shoot, I'll go. I've never seen a live play like that before."

"Okay, we'll be leaving at six o'clock. See you later," Debbie said, and she hung up.

I held on to the phone for a minute, starting to regret my decision. Twenty dollars was a fortune and more money than I had at the moment. I'd just spent half my baby-sitting income on a down payment for a tennis racket.

"You through with the phone?" my brother Larry said, popping his head into the kitchen. Larry was fifteen years old and just starting to live on the phone.

"No. I'm gonna call Debbie back and tell her I can't go."

"Go where?"

"To the dinner theater to see an actor who used to be on a soap opera."

"Which one? *Guiding Light*?"

"No, *Another Love*." I dialed Debbie's number, but the line was busy, so I hung up.

"Let me have it," Larry said.

"Oh, okay, but don't take long—I have to call her back." I moved away from the phone and went into the family room. My parents were watching TV. My dad had the dog in his lap, and my mother was crocheting.

"Who called?" Mama said.

"Debbie." I sighed and sank down in my seat.

"What'd she want?"

"Oh, she just wanted to know if I could go to the dinner theater on Tuesday with her and everybody to see their favorite soap opera star perform in a play."

"That sounds like fun. Are you going?"

"I don't know how in the world I can. I can't afford it."

"What happened to all your baby-sitting money?"

"I spent it for a down payment on a tennis racket."

"On a tennis racket?" She looked at me like she couldn't understand why anybody in the world would do such a thing.

"I know, it was stupid!" I said. I felt embarrassed. I'd only done it because I'd read in a *Cosmopolitan* magazine article that you should play tennis if you wanted to meet a wealthy man.

Mama kept looking at me.

"I said it was stupid!" I said. "I'm sorry about it now!"

She went back to her crocheting.

"I do wish I could see that show," I said after a moment. "I wish I could afford it."

Mama didn't respond.

"I wish I had a real job," I said.

"You can look for one, can't you?" she said softly.

"You don't think I do? I read the want ads every day!"

"Maybe you're too picky."

"Picky, my eye. Unless you call not wanting to work in some sock factory from midnight to seven being picky!"

Mama shook her head as she studied her crocheting. I

could tell she wasn't eager to get into an argument with me, but this made me all the more grouchy. "Larry, get off the phone, darn it!" I hollered. "I have to call Debbie back and tell her I can't go to that play!"

"Hush," my dad said, turning to look at me for the first time.

"Well, tell him to get off the daggone phone! He's always on that thing!" I jumped up and headed for the kitchen.

"Calm down," my dad said, raising his voice, which he hardly ever did.

This caused me to really lose my temper. I whirled around and yelled, "Well, what in the world do you want me to do? Install my own phone?"

Daddy stared at me with a deadpan expression, then he went back to his program. Mama bowed her head over her crocheting. The dog was the only one who kept looking at me, and his expression was reproachful.

"We'll give you the money to go to the dinner theater," my mother said after a moment.

"Oh, you don't have to do that," I said. But I knew they would, and I knew I'd let them. To save what little dignity I had left, I went on back to my room.

2

The dinner theater was ten miles away at the big indoor mall outside Summerville. It was on the main level across from Kinney Shoes and Waterbed City. Ida Faye, Debbie, Boyd, and I got there around six-thirty. Boyd picked up the tickets while we women waited on a bench in the mall promenade.

"I brought a sweater in case the air conditioning's too cold," Debbie said loudly. "What about y'all?"

"Well, I have this." Ida Faye showed Debbie the jacket of her red pants suit hanging across her arm. Ida Faye loved the color red.

"What about you, Sunny?" Debbie said.

"I forgot to bring anything."

"I hope you won't regret that."

"Don't worry, I won't."

Debbie was really irritating me lately with this efficient attitude of hers. She'd changed since she and Boyd had gotten married last Christmas. We used to be right good friends, but these days she needled me a lot, like she was jealous that I was still single or something. I'll agree Ray's brother Boyd was pretty dull. Ida Faye and Ray were the ones with all the charm and talent in that family.

When Boyd joined us, Debbie asked him if he had the tickets, even though they were in plain view.

"What d'you think these are?" Boyd said. "You ready to see this play, Grandma?" he asked Ida Faye loudly.

"I reckon," she said.

"At these prices we sure hope it's good, don't we, Grandma?" Debbie nearly shouted. I wished they'd quit all that yelling; Ida Faye could hear as good as anybody.

Suddenly the doors to the theater opened and a glamorous-looking woman in a low-cut dress exclaimed, "We're open!"

All of us followed her into a softly lit lobby where the air smelled like the pages of an old book. On the wall were photographs of the actors. "That's Joe," Ida Faye said, pointing at a man's picture, but I was too caught up in the general excitement to take much notice.

The lady in the low-cut dress tore our tickets in half. "How are you folks tonight?"

"Fine," we all said; then we went down a carpeted

hallway and entered the theater. An usher led us up to our table and one of the waitresses poured our water. She was buxom and had feathered brown hair. "Y'all can get your plates down there and serve yourselves," she said.

We thanked her and headed down to the food. "Oh, my word," Ida Faye said.

There was an amazing amount of food on two long buffet tables: roast beef, green and pink Jell-O salads, peas, potatoes, beets, turkey, chicken legs. We piled our plates high, then walked back up to our table. The atmosphere in the theater was like a big party—people jabbering and laughing; the waitresses sashaying around serving drinks and pouring coffee.

Our waitress finally cleared our plates away. "I'm so stuffed, I'm about to pop. How about y'all?" Debbie said.

We all said we were stuffed too.

The waitresses rolled away the buffet tables, and a few minutes later the lights flickered and everyone started to quiet down. The theater got darker and darker. You could hear a few people coughing and something being moved across the stage in the dark.

Soft violin music started playing and the lights came up on a house. It had a sign on it that said: "Dixieland—Rooms and Board." It was like a real house sitting right there on the stage, except half of it was cut away so you could see the inside. A man was sitting writing at a desk. He had dark brown curly hair and wore a white collarless shirt and gray trousers. Debbie squeezed my elbow. "That's him!" she said.

I'd figured it must be.

The music grew softer and a train whistle blew and Joe Brady began talking: "My brother Ben's face is like a piece of slightly yellow ivory. His high, white forehead is knotted fiercely by an old man's scowl. His mouth is like a knife. His smile the flicker of light across the blade."

I don't know what came over me, but I felt like bursting into tears. I didn't know if it was Joe Brady that was killing me or the poetry he was saying, but it was as if I was swept away hearing him go on like that about his brother Ben.

When he finished talking, he kept writing, and the other actors and actresses began to act down on the front porch, but I didn't pay any attention to what they were saying. I couldn't take my eyes off Joe Brady.

When the lights for the intermission came on, it was all I could do to mumble, "Bathroom. . . ." I slid out of my seat and headed to the lobby, right to Joe Brady's photograph. He was smiling with beautiful white teeth showing; tree leaves and sunlight were behind his head. I stood there with my eyes glued to the picture till the lights in the lobby blinked, and the woman in the low-cut dress said it was time to go back inside.

In the second part, Joe—or his character, who was named Eugene—wanted to go to college, but there wasn't any way the family could afford it. He got in a fight with his mother, and the next thing you knew his brother Ben got sicker and sicker till he died. When Ben died it was one of the most moving things I'd ever experienced. I had to bite my napkin to keep from making crying noises. After Ben's death, Eugene tried to get his girlfriend Laura to run off with him, but she wasn't interested in that.

At the end of the play, Eugene talked to his dead brother Ben. He said, "I want the world. Where is the world?" I knew just how he felt, so you can imagine how I nearly fell off my chair when Ben answered, "The world is no where, no one, Gene. *You* are your world."

The train whistle blew and the show was over. I clapped and clapped till I was about the last one in the theater to quit. As Debbie and Boyd got up to go, they were talking about something, but I wasn't paying attention. "Sunny," Debbie said.

"What?"

"I said we're going backstage."

"What for?"

"To see if Joe Brady'll autograph all our programs."

"Well, y'all go—I'll wait here."

"How come?"

"I'm shy."

"I've never known *you* to be shy," Debbie said.

"Well, I am today. You take my program and get him to sign it, okay?"

Debbie took my program. "All right, chicken," she said, and the three of them headed down the steps.

I probably would have gone backstage another time, but after what I'd just experienced it seemed tacky to stomp back there with a whole group and demand Joe Brady's autograph. As the theater emptied out, I watched the waitresses scurrying around the room, stripping the soiled linen off the tables.

On the ride home Debbie said Joe Brady had been real sweet and was just as good-looking up close. "I think he took a shine to Grandma," Boyd said loudly, teasing Ida Faye.

Apparently Joe had kissed Ida Faye on the cheek. He'd also signed all our programs *Best Wishes, Joe Brady*. His capital *B*, *W*, *J*, and *B* were dramatic and swooping. "I think his signature's right sexy," Debbie said. I agreed it was.

Later when I was in bed, I kept thinking about Joe Brady. I was so keyed up I couldn't sleep. I heard the train whistle blow in my head and I heard Joe say, "My brother Ben's face is like a piece of . . ." but darned if I could remember what it was like a piece of.

I was so restless I finally got out of the bed and got my little tape player. I lay back down, and as I played some slow songs, I imagined Joe was standing in my doorway.

"Sunny, did you call me?" my imagination said.

"Yes," I answered.

He started walking across the floor till he stood by my bed and looked down at me. "My wife Sunny's face is like a piece of the sun," Joe Brady, my dream, said softly.

3

The next day Joe Brady was still strongly on my mind as I drove downtown to answer a help wanted ad at McKay's Dime Store. I was wearing the same dress I'd worn the night before to the dinner theater—an orange clingy nylon dress that had belonged to Debbie before she'd gained so much weight.

As I strode around McKay's, I observed that the saleswomen were mostly short and fat and had beauty-parlor-styled hair. I wandered over to the cosmetics section and stood there awhile to get a feel for what it would be like to work in a place like this. I found myself paying attention to a couple of young girls talking about the flavored lipsticks. "You think Mike'll like grape?" one said.

"I don't know. Try this peach-smelling one," the other said.

They giggled, and then one of them glanced in my direction and caught me watching them. I guess I was wishing I was young again and that I didn't have to worry about finding a job, especially in a depressing place like this. I grabbed a pair of fingernail scissors, paid for them at the register, then fled from the store.

Boy, it hadn't taken me long to discover that I'd be real unhappy working in a place like that. I had no idea what to do next as I drove down the highway. I stared guiltily at the fast food restaurants beside the road. I suspected I wouldn't have much trouble getting a job in one of them, but the thought of that sort of chilled me. I could just see myself in a little yellow hat calling hamburger orders into a microphone for a bunch of mean-spirited teenagers.

Actually, no place in Wheeler seemed like a good place to work. The nearest excitement was out at the Summerville Mall, where the dinner theater was. It occurred to me for the first time that maybe I should check out some of the stores there.

I drove on out to the mall and parked in the giant parking lot. As I headed to the front entrance, I caught sight of myself in the glass door. Boy, did I look goofy in my orange dress. I hoped Joe Brady wouldn't see me. Of course, I knew I was being silly—he'd have no earthly idea who I was. I seriously doubted that Debbie had said to him last night, "Oh, you know, Joe, I have a skinny blond friend named Sunny who's a little on the short side and often wears an orange clingy nylon dress. Keep an eye out for her."

Waterbed City didn't need any new employees. But next door at Kinney Shoes they at least gave me an application to fill out. I sat down on a bench in the indoor promenade and got to work on it.

I was doing the address part of the form when a familiar voice said, "Hey, you."

It was Ray. "Hey, you, yourself!" I said, laughing. I was real glad to see him. "What are you doing here?"

"I came to get Grandma's blood-pressure pills. Boyd forgot 'em last night." He indicated the little bag he was carrying.

"Well, sit down and visit—I'm lonely," I said, pulling on his arm.

"No, I got to get back."

"Oh, go on and go then. . . ." I pushed his arm away. "You're always taking off."

"Okay, just for a minute," he said. He sat down beside me and lit a cigarette. His fingernails were black from working on cars. "What's that?" he said.

"A Kinney's job application."

"You want to work there?" He sounded disbelieving.

"Well, not particularly. But it's about time I got a job, wouldn't you say?"

"Well, I don't know about you selling shoes, Sunny."

"Then what do you suggest I do?"

Ray shrugged. "I don't know—be useless like me."

"Oh, you're not useless. You help a lot of people by fixing their cars."

He looked away from me and took a puff on his cigarette. I figured Ray was wishing he was off playing music somewhere and not living at home at all. I wondered if he was afraid to be a performer again.

"Seriously, what kind of a job do you think I should try to do?" I said.

"Do something you like."

"That's easier said than done. I'm not even sure what I like."

Ray didn't say anything.

"And if I knew what I liked, I bet I wouldn't be able to get a job doing it!"

Ray just took a drag off his cigarette and looked down at the floor. It was hard to get much out of him sometimes.

"In fact, I know I wouldn't be able to," I said, egging him on.

He raised his head and stared at the box office at the dinner theater not far away from us. "I heard y'all had a great time last night," he said.

"We did. So what?" I was perturbed at him for taking away all my enthusiasm for working at Kinney's and then changing the subject.

"Why don't you ask for a job there?"

"Where?"

"At the dinner theater."

I blew air out of my nostrils. "Oh, sure, Ray."

"Why not?"

"Can't you see me onstage right now?"

"What about working as a waitress?" he said.

"Get serious."

"What's wrong with that?"

"You know I've never waitressed before!"

"Oh, and you've sold shoes?" He stretched. "Okay, go ahead. I don't mind. Spend your time pinching people's toes. . . ." He laughed.

"Well, what in the world do you want me to do?" I said. "Just walk in there and say, 'Hey, y'all! Let me be a waitress!' "

"That's what you did just now at Kinney's."

"There's a difference!"

"The only difference I see is that you'd really like to have one of those two jobs."

"Oh, for crying out loud, Ray."

"Okay, have it your way." He stood up. "I've got to get these pills home." He whapped my head with his bag. "See you later, sunshine."

"Good riddance." I watched him walk away. Then I wadded up my Kinney application and tossed it in the waste can. I sat down again and stared at the box office. When the line of ticket buyers dwindled down, I got up and walked over to the window.

"Can I help you?" the girl said.

I leaned down close to the little opening and said, "You have a waitress application?"

The girl reached under the counter. "Here," she said, handing me a form. "Fill it out and bring it back." She gave me a pen, and I thanked her and headed back to my bench. This'll show Ray, I thought. I knew they wouldn't hire me in a million years, but at least I could tell him I'd tried.

I sat down and got to work. When I came to job experience, I wrote: "None, except baby-sitting. This required preparing and serving meals to children of all ages."

When I carried my application back to the girl in the box office, a short slick-haired man was standing there with her. The girl took my form and handed it to him. He glanced at it, then said, "Would you like to come in and talk?"

"What, now?" Hadn't he read that I'd had no waitress experience?

But he just nodded.

"Well, okay," I said.

He came around and opened the door for me, and I followed him back to an office off the lobby of the theater. He motioned for me to sit down; then he sat behind a large desk and began reading over my application. "So," he said, "you've served meals to children of all ages?"

I couldn't tell if he was making fun of me or not. "Just about," I said.

He laughed and stared at me for a moment. "How would you like to assist the other waitresses?" he said.

"Assist them?"

"I'm sorry, but I can't let you start off cocktail waitressing right away—"

"Oh, no, I don't mean I mind assisting them—I'd love to assist them!" I laughed. "I'm just so shocked you'd want to hire me!"

"Is there any reason I shouldn't?"

"No sir! Except I'm not very experienced, but Lord, if you don't mind, I sure don't!" I laughed again—I knew I was sounding like an idiot, but I was so thrilled, I couldn't help it. "Well, when do I start?"

"Well, how about tonight? Can you come back around five-thirty?"

"Of course!"

"Do you have a black skirt and a white blouse?"

"Yes I do—I mean I've got the skirt, but I'll have to borrow a blouse from my neighbor Debbie. She's heavier than me, but it'll probably be okay—" I put my hand over my mouth to make myself be quiet.

But the man didn't seem to mind. "Good," he said. He stood up. "It's nice to meet you, Sunny. My name's Ed Swank."

"Thank you, Mr. Swank," I said. "I appreciate it. I'll see you in a few hours."

We said good-bye and I let myself out of the office. I flew down the promenade and out of the mall. It wasn't until I was driving on the interstate that it really hit me. I started trembling and grinning and saying, "Oh wow! Oh wow! Oh wow!"

When I turned onto my street, I bypassed our house

and drove up the hill to Ida Faye's. Before I was even all the way in her driveway, I cut off my engine and jumped out of the car. "Ray! Ray!" I shouted as I charged up to the porch.

Ray stepped out his front door.

"Guess what!" I yelled, scrambling up the steps. "I got a job at the dinner theater! I'm gonna assist the waitresses —starting tonight!"

"Hey," he said, grinning. "Isn't that something?"

"Yes!" I threw my arms around him and hugged him real tight. "Thank you!" I said. I could feel him stiffen a little. I guess I hadn't hugged Ray this close since I was a tiny child.

4

At five-thirty I arrived back at the mall. I was wearing Debbie's white blouse and a black skirt. Debbie's blouse was so big on me, I thought I looked a little pathetic in it, and my hair was bad too—it needed a trim. But who cared? I was too excited to care.

One of the waitresses showed me around the theater. Her name was Donna. She was the large-bosomed girl who'd waited on all of us the night before. She introduced me to the other two waitresses, Jennifer and Tracy, and to the cook in the kitchen, whose name was Beth.

"You'll work at my station," Donna said. "Before the show starts, I'll be taking orders for cocktails for the intermission. You pour water and get coffee for people. Here's the cream and sugar bowls—"

I took notes on a yellow legal pad.

"Make two pots of coffee," Donna said as she filled a coffee cone. "And when they get low, marry them."

"Marry them?"

"The coffee—put what's left in the two pots together."

"Oh, that's cute," I said, laughing, and I wrote that down.

Next Donna pushed some buttons on the coffee machine and the water began to trickle down. "Make sure there's always water or coffee in the pot, or it'll crack. We don't want that to happen."

"I guess not!" I said.

We sat down at a table with Jennifer and Tracy and started helping them dry the silverware and fold the napkins. I only heard snatches of their conversation as I dried the knives. My head was swimming with all the details I'd just learned. I wasn't sure which buttons I was supposed to push for coffee—and where did I get the ice for the water pitchers and what had Donna told me about the tea bags? Now and then I put a knife down and scribbled a question on my yellow legal pad.

"What are you writing?" Tracy said.

"Just some questions," I said.

"Let's hear them," Donna said.

I read off all my questions. The girls got a kick out of them, and the chunky blond one named Jennifer said, "Hell, she makes even me feel smart." Before I could get mad, she said she was only kidding, and then she went on to help answer my questions. When I'd finished going over everything I'd written down with them, I actually felt pretty confident.

But I got nervous all over again watching the audience enter the theater. Donna handed me a wet aluminum water pitcher and told me to go pour. My hand was pretty shaky and I poured silently for the first people, but gradually I got more control. "How are y'all tonight?" I asked my third table.

"Fine, just fine," the couple answered.

"Good," I said.

By the time I'd finished pouring all my water, I was ready to take on something more complicated. I served a couple of Sankas, which involved placing the little orange packets next to the teapots. Then I took cream and sugar to the tables. Everything was fine till a woman asked for Sweet'n Low. I hurried to my station and searched frantically for it. "What are you doing?" Donna asked as she passed by me.

"Looking for the Sweet'n Low!"

"There it is—in the basket."

"Thanks! You're a lifesaver!"

I was so preoccupied with doing my job right that I nearly forgot what was about to happen here. It all came back in a jolt when Donna said, "Tell 'em last call for drinks. Show's starting in ten minutes."

I dashed around clearing the tables; then I helped the other girls carry out the dirty dishes. After that I asked

Donna if it would be okay if I watched the play. She told me to go ahead, but to be ready to help at the intermission.

I positioned myself in the back of the theater just as the lights were starting to go out. I could hear the boarding house being rolled across the stage. Then the violin music started and the lights came on . . . and there he was. Joe Brady. He looked about as good as I'd remembered. "My brother Ben's face is like a piece of slightly yellow ivory. . . ." From then on, I was a goner.

Near the end of the first act Donna came and got me. I followed her out to the bar area, where the girls were preparing their intermission drinks. I helped put ice in the glasses, then snuck off and peeked into the theater just in time to see the last moment in the act, when Joe and his girlfriend in the play are together. Joe said, "It might rain," and Laura said, "I love the rain." Tears filled my eyes as the lights slowly went out.

When the play was over, I helped strip the dirty linen off the tables. It seemed like a miracle to me that just yesterday I'd observed the other girls doing this, and today I was right here doing it with them.

After we finished, Donna came up to me and said, "Sunny, here's some money from my tips. I'm sorry it's not more, but it was a slow night."

"That's okay," I said. "I appreciate it." It was only two dollars, but I didn't think that was half bad, considering I was also making the minimum hourly wage. "Oh," I said, catching her before she walked off. "I was wondering—do y'all ever see the actors offstage?"

"Sure, they walk through here every night."

"They do? Do you ever talk to them?"

"Sure, lots," Donna said.

"Oh, wow."

I waited for a little while, but none of the actors appeared. I was just getting ready to leave when the two women who played the mother and the girl Laura walked out from the backstage area. As I watched them head out of the theater, I was surprised to see that Laura looked right plain in real life. You'd never have guessed she was anyone special. Suddenly my stomach turned over—Joe Brady was coming out. Now with him it was a different story. He really did look like a star. His dark curly hair fell down over his forehead, and his arms were tanned and sinewy.

Donna and Jennifer called out to him. He smiled and waved at them. When he passed by me, he caught my eye. "Hi," he said.

"Hi." My voice was barely audible.

He held my gaze for a couple of seconds; then he headed on out of the theater.

The look he'd given me nearly knocked me over. Before you knew it, I was taking off after him. I felt like I couldn't stop myself—I was like that girl in *The Red Shoes,* the old movie about the girl whose shoes made her dance even when she didn't want to. I followed Joe all the way down the hall and out through the theater lobby to the promenade. I watched him turn to the right; then before I made a fool of myself, I forced my feet to go left, and I headed on out to my car.

When I got home, I told my family every detail about work that evening.

"Well, I'm glad you got a job you like," was all my mother had to say.

"Yeah, that's good," my dad said, and he went back to stroking the dog and watching the news.

They were the opposite of people who make a big deal about things.

5

Each day at the dinner theater was better than the day before. I got to where I could pour water and make coffee with my eyes closed practically, and the money I was making improved, too—I made five dollars in tips both Friday and Saturday nights.

Every night after the show I'd wait around until Joe Brady would walk through the theater. I watched Donna, Jennifer, and Tracy call out things to him, and sometimes he'd stop and talk to them for a minute.

I never got up the nerve to say anything more than hi to him, but believe me I got a lot of mileage out of that hi. Before I went to work, I took forever putting on my makeup and fixing my hair, imagining how I'd look when he passed by me and we both said hi.

Sunday morning I went over to Debbie's to have my hair shaped. When I was a child, Ray used to say my hair was like a little old rabbit's tail—that's how curly it was.

I sat on the porch steps with a towel around my neck while Debbie worked on me. Ray and Ida Faye had come over and were sitting with us. Boyd wasn't there. He was working at the Winn Dixie in Taylorsville, where he'd recently been made the assistant store manager. Everyone seemed enthusiastic about my job, though Debbie actually appeared to be a little jealous.

"Just what do you do besides pour water?" she said, pressing a ball of curls into my hand. She was making me hold my hair so it wouldn't blow across her yard.

"Not much, but I might learn how to serve cocktails," I said.

"Oh, no. . . ." Ida Faye clucked her tongue. She was a Baptist.

"It's okay, Grandma," Ray said. "If Sunny wasn't there to do it, somebody else would be."

"What's the news in your papers this week?" I asked Ida Faye to get her mind off the alcohol. Ida Faye enjoyed reading those kinds of papers you get at the checkout counter at the supermarket. Ray and I liked to tease her about it.

"Well, one of 'em says that Jackie Gleason's seen aliens—"

Ray and I burst out laughing.

"Well, I didn't say I believed it," Ida Faye said.

When Debbie was finished, she shook out the towel and handed me a mirror.

"It looks good," Ida Faye said.

I glanced at Ray. He was just staring at me and sort of smiling.

"Thanks, Debbie." I looked down at my watch. "Whoops," I said, standing. "I better get a move on—we have a matinee today."

"Sounds like she thinks she's the star of the show," Debbie said. That was the most spiteful thing she'd said all day, but I guess it wasn't that bad.

That afternoon between the matinee and the evening show, Donna and Jennifer asked if I wanted to go with them to Lacy's, a punk-style bar and restaurant in the mall. The two of them seemed to get a kick out of my company lately—they sort of treated me like I was their little mascot.

"Sure," I said. "But I only have a few dollars—I'll have to just get a Coke or iced tea."

Just then Joe Brady and John Wells walked out from backstage. John Wells was the man who played Ben in the play. In real life he seemed to be sort of a sweet, shy man. He was originally from Canada, the program said.

"Hey, there go two good-looking guys," Jennifer said to me and Donna. She said it loud enough for the men to hear. She and Donna were always saying things like that. I thought you had to admire their nerve. Of course, they were both over twenty-one years old and not what you'd call inexperienced. Donna was even divorced and had a one-year-old daughter.

Joe and John glanced at the three of us and smiled.

"Have y'all ever been to Lacy's?" Donna called out.

Joe shook his head. "Where is it?" he said. I felt he was just asking to be polite.

"Go to the other end of the mall near Sears, turn left, go up the stairs, walk down to Friday's, and it's across the way next to the Butterfly Boutique."

Joe and John looked at each other and laughed, as if they were confused. "I guess you'll have to show us sometime," Joe said, and he started to move along.

"When?" Jennifer said.

Joe smiled good-naturedly and said, "Whenever you want."

"Well, where are y'all going now?" Jennifer said.

"I don't know," Joe said.

"Then come on and join us—we're going there."

Joe looked at John like he didn't know how they were going to get out of this.

"Come on!" Jennifer said.

The men laughed and said something to each other, then Joe said, "Okay."

"All right!" Jennifer said.

The five of us started out of the theater together. Jennifer maneuvered herself till she was walking right beside Joe Brady. She asked him how he liked this area, and had he ever been to North Carolina before. Donna asked John Wells where he was from originally. She knew as well as I did that John was from Montreal, Canada.

I walked alongside Donna and John, but I kept my eye on Joe and Jennifer walking up ahead. It looked like she was talking his ear off. Jennifer had broad shoulders and short, straight, blond hair, and a moon-shaped face. I'd always considered myself pretty outgoing, but next to her I felt like a wimp.

When we got to Lacy's, Joe and John looked at the menu posted outside. Loud music was blaring from inside. The men talked to each other for a minute, and then Joe said, "I don't think we'll eat here today."

"It's too noisy," John explained.

"Well, I don't know any other good places," Jennifer said.

"How about that Greek place?" John asked Joe quietly. He pointed to a small restaurant down the concourse.

"Sure, why not?" Joe said. "Thanks anyway," he said to us; then he and John started to take off. But then Joe stopped—he must have felt bad with the three of us just standing there, staring longingly after them. "You girls want to join us?" he said.

"Sure!" Jennifer and Donna said together, and of course I stepped right up with them.

At the Greek restaurant, we all squeezed around a table for four. I got wedged in between Joe and Jennifer. I hoped this didn't make her mad, but it wasn't my fault—

Joe had put the chair between him and Jennifer when it looked like there wasn't going to be a place for me to sit.

I didn't say a word as Donna and Jennifer chatted away. They were asking Joe all kinds of questions about his soap opera.

When the waitress came to the table and started taking orders, I checked in my pocketbook to see exactly how much money I had—just two dollars and fifty cents. Ordinarily between shows I'd have eaten for free in the kitchen of the dinner theater. When the waitress got to me, I said, "A dinner salad, please."

"Is that all?" she said.

"Yes ma'am." Right after I said *ma'am,* an awful thing happened. I swallowed the wrong way and I started coughing. It was one of those terrible throat-tickling coughs that makes you feel like you're going to die. I couldn't stop. Donna and Jennifer kept asking, "You okay? You okay?"

Of course I couldn't answer them. I don't know why people always ask you that when you're choking. Tears were coming out of my eyes and my face was on fire. Joe handed me a glass of water. I took a few sips, and that helped, but when I got some control and tried to laugh it off, I started to choke again. I sipped more water till I finally recovered. I was so relieved when the attention left me—it had been mortifying having everyone watch me cough.

But when I glanced over at Joe Brady, I caught him

still staring at me—it was as if he'd just woken up to the fact I was alive. I looked away and dried my eyes with my napkin, praying my face wasn't all smeared with mascara.

After a few seconds I stole another glance at Joe. I was surprised to see he was still looking at me. Whatever in the world for? I wondered, but I just smiled at him.

"What's your name," he asked softly.

"Sunny Dickens," I said. I started picking apart the napkin in my lap.

"Really? Hey, John, listen to this great name—Sunny Dickens. Good stage name, huh?"

John Wells nodded as he looked at me. "I like her hair too," he said to Joe as if I wasn't there. "It looks like lamb's wool."

"It's more like a rabbit's tail," I said.

Joe laughed. "It's nice. Can I touch it?"

"Sure, go ahead."

He gently pressed his hand against my hair. My heart stopped. "Wow, it *feels* like lamb's wool," he said.

"I don't know," I said, feeling short of breath. "I never felt a lamb."

He laughed again. He really seemed to like my jokes.

Suddenly Jennifer got Joe's attention by asking him something about the soap opera. That was okay with me —I needed a moment to calm down. My napkin was in shreds.

After a while the dinners came. Joe eyed my little salad. "That's not much food, Sunny," he said.

"Oh, it's fine," I said.

"You want some of my souvlaki?" he said.

"No, thank you. I'm fine, thank you." I glanced at the other girls. They were digging into their shish kebabs, and not very attractively.

The rest of the meal, Jennifer and Donna kept Joe and John busy asking them questions. Even though Joe didn't talk to me, I was sure he was aware of me. A few times he looked at me and just stared; and later, on the walk back to the theater, he glanced over his shoulder as Jennifer was talking to him. Not until he caught my eye and smiled did he turn back to Jennifer.

I was so thrilled about getting all this attention, I didn't hang around that night after the show. I hurried home with my joy before anything could come along and wreck it. After I got into bed and turned out my light, I luxuriated in my memories. I kept touching my hair to feel how it had felt to Joe Brady, and I said my name out loud to hear how it had sounded to him.

6

The dinner theater was closed on Mondays, so I didn't have to go to work the next day. By the time I got up, the house was empty. I walked into the kitchen and the dog yapped and hopped around my feet, his toenails clicking against the floor. "Beat it," I said. I never had much patience with him.

As I ate my cereal, Joe Brady was all that I thought about. I wondered what he was doing on his day off. I knew he and all the actors lived in apartments close by the mall and they ate at restaurants at the mall. If I went out there I just might bump into him, I thought. I needed to do some shopping anyway; I wanted to buy a blouse that fit. What a good idea this was! I nearly fell over the dog in my haste to get going. "Move, you fool," I said.

I took a shower, then fluffed out my hair. I put on my gold-flecked tube top and a pair of tight jeans, and I got my tip money out of my top drawer. Twenty-three dollars. Not bad, I thought, considering it didn't even include my paycheck. I'd collect my pay every Wednesday, starting this week. I still could hardly believe my good luck in getting this job. The day I'd discovered the dinner theater had been the first day of a whole new life for me—everything before that day seemed pale now in comparison.

Even riding a bus was a special event now. Ray was working on my mother's car today, so she'd borrowed mine to take to the dry cleaners where she worked. As I rode the bus to the mall, I pretended Joe was with me and I pretended to be showing him things. I pointed out Lyman Park to him and I showed him Ida Faye's church. I'd visited there with her several times. I always got a kick out of the preacher. He was a funny little man named Reverend Putt who seemed more concerned with picnics and hot-dog suppers than with people's sins. Ida Faye told me that at the last service Reverend Putt had gotten so happy that he'd taken to dancing. I'd wondered if this meant he'd talked in tongues or something, but I didn't ask her.

I imagined having a discussion with Joe Brady about religion. I thought I'd like to tell him some of my personal theories. For instance, I believed Jesus wasn't necessarily a man, but was more like a spirit that lived inside everybody and everything. I'd never discussed this with anyone but Debbie. She'd said the idea sounded poetic. I'd told it to her the night before she'd gotten married—when she'd tearfully confessed to me that she wasn't a virgin and she was afraid she'd sinned against Jesus.

I'd explained my theory about Jesus at the time, and then to make her feel even better, I'd told her I wasn't a virgin either. Actually I was a virgin then—and I was still one now. At least in the technical sense. My last boyfriend, Buddy Willis, and I had gone steady for five months. We'd carried on quite a bit and most likely would have gone the whole distance, I think, if his family hadn't moved to Greenville last spring. Secretly his moving suited me fine. I mean, I was eager for experience, but Buddy wasn't my idea of the perfect first one. He was pretty immature for one thing. He'd once embarrassed me to death by getting real angry at a party because my makeup had gotten all over the shoulder and collar of his yellow shirt due to my perspiring when we'd danced. It wasn't like it wouldn't wash out, and Buddy had tons of shirts anyway because his father worked at one of the mills and got all the family's clothes at a big discount.

When I got to the mall, I scanned the parking lot for Joe Brady's green Volkswagen bug. I didn't see it, but that didn't really mean anything—the parking lot went all the way around to the other side.

I found the greatest blouse at Penney's. It was one-hundred-percent cotton and had pleats down the front of it and big puffy sleeves. After I paid most of my money for it, I had the saleswoman cut off the tags so I could wear it. I went back to the dressing room and dropped my gold tube top into my Penney's bag; then I primped a little before taking off.

I walked slowly down the promenade, keeping an eye out for Joe Brady and for any of the other actors. At one point I thought I saw the woman who played Laura in Baskin-Robbins, but I was wrong.

When I got close to the theater, I stopped at a pay phone and pretended to be looking up a number in the phone book. I put a quarter in the slot and dialed the number for Time. All this playacting gave me the opportunity to survey the area. I observed Linda, the girl who worked in the box office, talking to Mr. Swank. At one point she caught sight of me and waved. I waved back and pretended to be talking to someone on the phone as the recording kept giving me the time.

Finally I gave up. Shoot, I thought, it didn't appear that I was going to get to see Joe Brady on my day off. I hung up the phone and went out to the sunny concourse to catch my bus home. I sat on a bench in front of Penney's, clutching my shopping bag and staring down at the concrete. The bright sun hurt my eyes.

"It's Sunny Dickens," a soft, British-sounding voice said.

I looked up, shielding my eyes. Lord, I couldn't believe it. It was John Wells talking—and Joe Brady was standing right there beside him! "Oh, hey!" I blurted out.

"What's Sunny Dickens up to?" Joe Brady said. It was hard to see him in the bright sunlight.

"I was just doing some shopping," I said, standing up.

"What did you buy?" John said, pointing to my Penney's bag.

Before I could think, I reached into the bag and pulled out my old wadded-up gold tube top.

"Good grief," John said.

All three of us laughed. It struck me as being so funny I nearly got hysterical. Tears came out of my eyes.

"Oh, we've made her cry," John said.

"No, you didn't—" I gasped.

"Get hold of yourself!" John said dramatically, and he grabbed me by the shoulders. "We'll demand they give you your money back!"

Joe was laughing real hard at John's playacting.

Finally we all calmed down and I wiped my eyes—it seemed like I always had wet eyes around these two. "What are y'all doing here?" I said.

"We're going to see a movie," Joe said.

"Oh, you are? What movie?" I sounded brave, but it was all I could do to stand there; my legs were like rubber.

"We haven't decided yet," John said. "Why don't you come with us and give us your advice on what to see?"

"That's a great idea," Joe said.

"Who—me?" I said.

"Absolutely. She looks like a reliable critic, doesn't she?" John asked Joe.

"Yeah, she does," Joe said.

"Well, I don't know about that," I said. *Me* give the two of them advice on what movie to see? I didn't think I could even walk.

"Come on," John Wells said. He took me by the elbow and guided me toward the entrance of the mall. Joe walked on my other side. Before we entered the main doors, Joe said, "Oh, look," and he walked over to a pet store window. John and I joined him, and the three of us watched some little kittens wrestling in a box. I stole a peek at Joe—his expression was like a child's. When he caught me looking at him, he grinned. I smiled and turned back to the window. Boy, little kittens had never looked so good before!

When we got to the movie theaters, we examined the choices of what was playing—*Splash,* which we'd all seen; a Burt Reynolds movie that John had seen; and *Bambi*.

"What do you think?" John asked me.

"It doesn't seem like there's anything to see," I said.

"Wait, what about *Bambi*?" Joe said. I thought he was making a joke.

"You want to?" John asked him.

"Sure, I'd love to see it again," Joe said. I couldn't believe it—not only had he seen *Bambi* before, but he wanted to see it again. "Have you seen it?" he asked me.

"Can't say that I have."

"Oh, then you have to see it—you'll love it." He tugged on my sleeve. "C'mon—I'll buy your ticket."

"Well, okay." I laughed and walked with the two men over to the ticket booth.

Hardly anyone was in the theater. We chose seats in the middle, and I led the way down the row with Joe following after me, and then John. We sat down just as the advertisements were starting. Joe laughed hard at an ad for Billy Bub's Fords and at an ad for Ham 'n' Biscuit-ville. I wasn't sure why he was laughing, but I was eager to see more ads to try and figure it out. When the cartoons started, boy, if he didn't get a kick out of them, too! I myself hadn't enjoyed cartoons since I was a little kid. By the third Donald Duck cartoon, I was starting to see some of the humor in it, but not much.

When the movie began, I got off on another tangent altogether. I pictured Joe slowly turning to me and pulling me over to him and kissing me. I imagined his hands moving slowly up under my blouse—not clumsy like Buddy Willis's, but more gentle and experienced. I imagined our mouths opening and our tongues touching till we couldn't stand it another second and we had to hurry out of the theater and rush to his place and make love.

I snuck a glance at him, and oh, just looking at his profile, I'd have liked to grab hold of him then and there and made love with him on the spot. I sank down in my seat and clutched my hands together. I tried to concentrate on Bambi and his friends flitting through the woods, but I couldn't keep from carrying on like a sex maniac in my mind.

When the show was over, the three of us left the movie

theater and strolled down the promenade. John and Joe were discussing whether or not the early artists at Walt Disney had used psychedelic drugs. I didn't say anything, because I had no idea whether they had or not. When we got near the dinner theater, I waited till there was a lull in their conversation; then I broke in—"Well, I better get on home. Thank you for the movies."

The men stopped walking and looked at me. John Wells reached out and touched my head. "Her hair *is* soft," he said to Joe.

"I told you it was," Joe said.

I laughed and said, "Well, I'll see y'all—"

"Good-bye," John Wells said.

" 'Bye."

"Good-bye, pretty sunny day," Joe Brady said.

I waved, then turned and walked quickly away. I hurried down the concourse to the bus stop. A bus was just pulling in when I got there. I jumped on it and rode all the way home smiling, smiling, and smiling.

7

When I got in the house, I wanted to shout out that I was in love. Larry was watching a *Kojak* rerun. "Hey, bud," I said, tousling his hair as he tried to swat me. I went on into the kitchen and found my mother spooning dog food from a can. "Hey!" I said.

"Hey, where have you been?"

"You won't believe it! I went to the movies with a couple of the actors from the dinner theater show. One of them was Ida Faye's soap opera star, Joe Brady!"

"Is that so?"

"Yes, and you'll never guess what we saw!"

"It must have been awfully good from the look on your face."

"Well, I don't know about good. . . ." I giggled.

"What was it?"

"Would you believe *Bambi*?"

"*Bambi*?"

"Yep, he just seems to love cartoons and *Bambi* and stuff like that. He and this other actor, John Wells, didn't care at all for Lacy's Bar at the mall. You'd think that would be a New Yorker's style, wouldn't you? But he likes children's things, like these kittens we watched in a pet store window!"

Mama laughed. "Does he wear a Mickey Mouse watch?"

"No, but he probably has one," I said, laughing. "It wouldn't surprise me."

"He does sound unusual," Mama said as she put the dog dish on the floor.

"He is." I left her and went into the family room. "Hey, turkey, how's driver's ed.? Hit any poles yet?"

Larry grunted and shook his head.

"Guess what—I just saw *Bambi* with the actors from the dinner theater. They're from New York City." I stared at *Kojak* on the TV. "They probably know Telly Savalas, or at least know someone who knows him. Joe was—"

"Hey." Larry twisted his neck to look at me. "Can you tell me during the commercial?"

"Sure, remind me."

I floated back to my room and closed my door and put on some music. It was almost more than I could stand. I danced in front of my mirror, then I tried to recreate my departure from Joe and John to get an idea of what I had looked like. " 'Bye." I waved at my mirror and backed up. *Pretty sunny day*, Joe had called me. I twirled over to my bed and fell face down onto it. When I heard my dad's car drive up, I jumped up and went outside to greet him.

"Hey, baldy," I said, making a little joke—he really had a full head of hair.

"Howdy," he said as he picked the evening paper off the grass.

"How was your day?" I said.

"Fine. How was yours?"

"Wonderful!"

"Good." He walked up to the house, trying to read the headlines on the folded front page. He'd make a great character in some play, I thought. He sold light bulbs wholesale for a living, and when he wasn't working, he was happy watching TV or going to the American Legion. He loved to buy little kitchen gizmos like cucumber slicers and tuna mixers. We'd always tease him about his drawer full of useless gadgets. He also liked to collect old watches and clocks. He spent lots of time tinkering with them, and sometimes he could even make one work. My dad loved precision instruments. He often said that if he could afford it, he'd like to own a Mercedes Benz because it was such a perfect machine. But I wouldn't call him a frustrated person even if he didn't have everything he wanted. As Ray once said about my dad: "He acts like everything in his life is a plus."

I watched Daddy go into the house, then I decided to go up the street and find out what Ray and Ida Faye were up to. I was really in the mood to visit people. The sun was glistening through the maple trees and the leaves were shaking as I headed up the hill.

I found Ray standing in his yard talking to an old man. He raised his cigarette at me and went on talking. He seemed to be explaining something to the man about his car. I climbed the porch steps and sat in a chair.

The late sun danced on Ray's straight brown hair as his cigarette smoke rose into the pine branches overhead. The fellow he was talking with seemed to be missing his teeth. Ray didn't charge his customers much, so he got some mighty poor ones sometimes. He was awfully good to people like that. In fact, Ray was pretty good to everybody. When I was little—say about six and he was twelve —he'd baby-sit for me and Larry, and I remember he was so kind he'd even let us tie him up and torture him. I'd always had a big crush on him. But when I was just entering junior high, he'd left town to be a professional musician. He'd played at clubs all over the south with a band called the Country Playboys. When he wasn't on the road he'd lived in a big farmhouse outside Charlotte with some other members of the band. At some point he got hooked on drugs, and about a year ago he'd had to go into a hospital in Durham. Debbie told me that Ray had gotten "plum down in the gutter" on account of drugs. But after he got cured, he'd quit the band and moved back to Wheeler. He'd been making his living as a shade-tree mechanic ever since. I'd been overjoyed when Ray had come back home, even though it upset me that he often treated me as if I was the age I'd been when he'd left five years before.

The screen door opened behind me. "Hey," Ida Faye said. She came out on the porch and sat down in the porch swing.

"Hey," I said.

"It's a pretty day today, isn't it?" she said.

"Yes, it is." I watched her move back and forth in the swing. Then I sighed and looked back at Ray and the old man in the sunlight. "Sometimes I just love everything," I said.

"Sounds like you're in love with some*body*," Ida Faye said.

I looked back at her and couldn't help grinning. "What makes you say that?"

"You just seem it."

"Well, I am in love," I said.

She nodded. I knew she was too polite to ask who it was, but I felt like I owed it to her to tell her. "Guess who it is. Don't tell."

"Who?" she said.

"It's someone at the dinner theater," I said.

"Who?" she said again, but her look told me she already knew. After all, she'd loved Joe for a couple of years on the soap opera.

"Guess."

She smiled and said, "Joe Brady." Just the way she said his name made me love him about ten times more.

8

When I got to work the next day, Suzanne, the house manager, grabbed me on my way down the hall. She was in charge while Mr. Swank was out of town for a few days. "Sunny, darling; I need your help!" she said. Suzanne always called people "darling" or "dear" like she was an old-fashioned movie actress or something, and she always wore high-heeled shoes. "Tracy's sick and I need you to serve drinks!" she said.

"But I haven't been taught yet."

"Can't you get Donna or Jennifer to show you? I'm desperate!"

"Well, sure, if they don't mind."

"Good girl—that's super!" She gave me an order pad, and I hurried into the theater, looking for Donna and Jennifer.

I saw Donna stacking cups up at her station. "Help!" I cried, laughing as I climbed the steps. "I have to serve drinks tonight because Tracy's sick!"

Donna looked at me. "Who said?"

"Suzanne—just now—and eek—I don't know the first thing!"

"Suzanne's crazy," Donna said. She picked up her empty tray and brushed past me down the steps.

"But she's in charge while Mr. Swank's gone, and she said—"

"It takes time to learn," Donna said coldly, and she pushed open the door to the kitchen and disappeared inside.

I was stunned. What was the matter with Donna—did she think I was a threat to her job or something? A moment later Jennifer burst out of the kitchen carrying a stack of napkins.

"Jennifer!" I said. "Can you show me what I need to know about serving drinks?"

She didn't look at me as she sat down at a table and started folding the napkins.

"Well, can you?" I said, walking over to her.

She shook her head and popped the piece of gum she was chewing.

I couldn't believe she was acting ugly too. "What's

wrong? I'm not out to steal y'all's jobs, you know," I said.

Donna bounded out of the kitchen and asked Jennifer something about milk pitchers. Jennifer was starting to answer her when I interrupted. "Look—would y'all please just show me what to do?" I was close to tears.

"Oh, good Lord, don't go to pieces," Donna said. "Just give the bartender copies of your orders, and then set up your glasses."

"But what glasses do I use? There's about a million of them!"

"The rock glasses are for anything on the rocks," she said in a bored voice. "Collins glasses are for sours, unless someone wants them straight up, then use sour glasses. Put highballs in the highball glasses and liqueurs in cordials, except for amaretto, Kahlua, and sherry. They go in the sherry glasses."

It sounded like she was talking in a foreign language. "But how do I know which glass is which?" I said.

Donna blew out a puff of air, causing her feathered bangs to rise off her forehead. She looked at me and said, "You don't know anything about liquor, do you?"

"I know some."

"Well, it doesn't seem like you do."

"I might learn if y'all would just tell—"

"We're too busy now," Jennifer interrupted.

"Well then, you can just both go to hell," I said, and I walked away from them. I heard Jennifer snort.

"Just ask if you have problems once you take your orders," Donna called after me. She was probably afraid I was on my way to report their behavior to Suzanne. I wasn't. I just needed to get away. If I'd hung around them any longer, I would have pounced on them.

I made coffee at Tracy's station, then stood like a stone and waited for the doors to open. Donna walked by and asked if I'd filled my water pitchers, but I didn't answer her.

When the audience started coming in, I poured their waters and coffees, then I got my order pad and started asking them what they wanted to drink at the intermission. My first table ordered two grasshoppers and two pink squirrels. The next table ordered spritzers. The third table ordered two martinis, a Manhattan, and two whiskey sours—one of them without fruit. The last table ordered a couple of Cokes. I was in shock. The bar didn't open until a few minutes before the intermission. This meant I'd have very little time to set up my glasses, get all these different drinks from the bartender, deliver them, and collect the money.

For the first time I didn't enjoy the play. I was dreading the intermission so much, I began wishing I was anybody but myself. I hardly even paid attention to Joe tonight, I was so afraid of messing up and maybe losing my job.

As soon as the bar opened, we all gathered to begin preparing our drinks. Donna and Jennifer were going great guns passing their order slips to Ross, the bartender, then filling their glasses with ice and tossing in olives and cherries and things like that. I numbly gave my order slips to Ross, then I stepped aside to keep out of everyone's way.

"Hurry! Move your trays down!" Ross commanded us in a harsh whisper. He was a big, sweaty man who seemed to take his job real seriously. His belly jiggled as he shook an aluminum shaker close to his ear. I stared at all the glasses on the shelves next to the bar, not knowing where to begin.

"Where are the glasses for these drinks?" Ross said when he was ready to pour from the shaker. He held up one of my order slips.

"I don't know which glasses to use," I said in a whispery voice.

"Use those," Ross said, pointing.

"Which?"

"Those!"

"I can't tell what you're pointing at." I tried to stay calm so Ross would stay calm, but it didn't work. He slammed the shaker down on the bar and huffed over to the glass shelves. He grabbed a couple of globular glasses and carried them back to the bar and poured a light-green foamy liquid into them.

"C'mon, get your other glasses, girl!" he ordered me.

"But I don't know which ones to use."

"Oh, this is crazy! Donna, Donna, help her, will you?" he said.

"Oh, for Pete's sake," Donna said, and she snatched my orders from my hand and yanked my tray from me. Then she speedily set up the glasses and put ice in them. Ross poured the liquor and Donna added the cherries, orange slices, olives, and lemon peels. "Now you think you can deliver these by yourself?" she said sarcastically.

"Yeah, if you just move your butt out of my way," I said. I picked up the heavy tray and carried it into the theater.

I didn't have any earthly idea which drinks were which. Right away I blew it by giving the grasshoppers to the women who'd ordered the squirrels. After that I offered the drinks with the fruit in them to the couple who'd ordered spritzers. "But we ordered spritzers!" the pinch-faced woman whined.

"Well, what do spritzers look like?" I asked her.

"Don't you know?"

I wanted to sock her. "No, I don't."

"That's okay," her husband said. "It's those, I think." I told him to please take the drinks off the tray.

"What's her problem?" the woman said as I moved away from their table.

"Those look like our martinis," a man at the next table called out. He must have been watching all the confusion. I handed him the drinks with the olives in them, then I started to leave. "Hold on there, doll, where's our whisky sours and Manhattan?" he said.

I gave him the last three drinks on my tray.

"Whoops!" he said. "You'll have to take this one back, I'm afraid. It has fruit in it."

"Well, just fish it out please," I said, and I walked away from the table.

"What a nut," I heard the man say.

"Miss, where's our Cokes?" someone hollered.

"Coming!" I veered down the steps and went around the corner to a deserted alcove in the back. I felt like I was going to pass out, I was so hot. I picked a program off the floor and fanned myself with it.

After resting a minute, I drank some water at the water fountain, then I went back out to the bar to get my Cokes. It was deserted now except for the cook, Beth, who was getting a beer. She smiled at me. "How's it going, Sunny?"

"Better not ask." I squirted Coke into two glasses. I didn't know if they were the right glasses or not. At that point I didn't care.

"Hey, is it true you dated Joe Brady?" Beth said.

I stopped squirting. "What?"

"Did you date Joe Brady yesterday?"

"Where'd you hear that?"

"Linda told us before work."

"Told who? Who'd she tell?"

"Me and Donna and Jennifer."

"Oh, well, it wasn't really a date," I said. I finished with my Cokes and carried them into the theater. So Donna and Jennifer were being nasty to me because they thought I'd dated Joe Brady—how low could they get? I didn't even feel like trying to explain the truth to them.

I delivered my Cokes and collected money for all the

drinks. Then I went into the kitchen and pressed a wet cloth to my face. I was starting to feel nauseous.

"What's wrong?" Beth said.

"I feel nauseous," I said.

"You want to sit down?"

"No, I think I want to leave. Could you bus my tables after the show?"

"What about Donna and Jennifer?"

"No, I don't want to ask them. You can keep my tips, except I don't expect to make much."

"Sure, that's all right, go on," Beth said.

I thanked her for helping me out; then, without saying anything else to anybody, I grabbed my pocketbook and fled from the theater.

I felt better as soon as I started for home. It was only nine-thirty when I turned onto our street, though, and I didn't really want to go in and have to explain why I'd left work early. I drove on past my house and slowed down when I got to Ida Faye's. Her house was dark, but I did see Ray's car in the driveway, and I thought I could make out the light of a cigarette on the front porch. I stopped my car and stuck my head out the window. "Ray?" I called out.

"Yeah," he said in the dark.

"What're you doing?"

"Nothing. Picking a little."

I got out of the car and headed up to his porch. "I thought you were working," he said. He was sitting on one of the steps holding his guitar.

"I freaked out at work," I said.

"What happened?"

"Some of the waitresses were being mean." I sat down on one of the steps below him.

He didn't say anything for a moment. "You want a beer?" he asked.

"Sure. You got a Miller Lite?"

"No, you'll have to take what I've got."

"Oh, well, anything's fine."

He stood up and went into the house. I picked up his guitar and played a couple of chords he'd taught me. I imagined I was playing a song and Joe Brady was watching me.

Ray came back out and handed me a beer. "Thanks. When are you gonna teach me some more chords?" I said.

"Anytime you want to learn."

"I always want to learn, but you're never around. Here." I handed him back his guitar. "Play that song you were learning a while ago about the cowboys and the babies."

He chuckled. " 'Mamas, Don't Let Your Babies Grow Up to Be Cowboys'?"

"Yeah, that's the one."

He started to play it. I loved to hear him sing, but he stopped after just a couple of lines and put his guitar down. "Why were the other waitresses mean to you?" he said. He was angry about it, I could tell. Ray talked real quietly whenever he was angry.

"Oh, they were jealous because they thought I'd been on a date with that soap opera star who's in the play."

"Why did they think that?"

"Just because I'd run into him and his friend at the mall yesterday and went to see *Bambi,* that's all. You couldn't call that a date."

"Bambi?"

"Yeah." I laughed a little. "He's got odd tastes."

"What did the other waitresses do that was so mean?" he said.

I told him the story about Donna and Jennifer refusing to help me and about the nightmare at the intermission and what all my customers had said to me and what I'd said back to them. When I finished talking, he crushed his beer can with his hand. "I'd like to get my hands on those two," he said. "You want another beer?"

"No, thanks, I haven't started this one yet."

"You want to borrow a book I've got on bartending?"

"Well, I don't think they're planning on making me the bartender, Ray," I said, laughing.

"No, no," he said, tapping me on the head. "I mean so you can learn the difference between things. It might help you when you serve drinks."

"Oh, well then, that sounds good. Yeah, I'd like to borrow it."

He got up and walked to the door. In the dark I heard him laugh. "Hey, why are you laughing?" I asked.

"You kill me sometimes," he said softly.

"Why?"

"Telling that man to fish the fruit out of his drink."

"Well, what about you? If I know you, you'd have poured it on his head!"

"Yeah, maybe back when I was crazy," he said. "But you—" He laughed again, then went on into the house.

I smiled to myself as I stared out at the dark. I felt a whole lot better now—I always did enjoy making Ray laugh.

9

I studied Ray's bartending book awhile before I went to bed and some more the next morning. He was right—it did help me learn the difference between things. A spritzer was just wine with some club soda in it, a whiskey sour was the drink with all the fruit, and grasshoppers were light green and were supposed to taste like peppermint. I figured I'd get Ross to teach me the different glasses tonight. Of course, that would only be necessary if Tracy wasn't back yet.

When I got to the theater, I was about to head into the ladies' room when I heard Donna's and Jennifer's voices coming from inside. I did an about-face and headed toward the kitchen. Ray had advised me to steer clear of those two—he knew what kind of temper I had.

I was just starting to fix coffee when Barry, one of the dishwashers, came up to me. "Hey, Barry," I said. "Is Tracy here tonight?"

"No, she's not coming in. Suzanne was looking for you."

"Why?"

"I don't know, but I heard that your job was in danger."

"What? Why?"

"Jennifer told Suzanne that you walked out on your customers last night."

"No! You're kidding."

"I heard her say you couldn't handle serving drinks so you just left."

"Oh, I don't believe this." I headed down the stairs and went straight back to the ladies' room and banged open the door. Jennifer was combing her hair in front of the mirror and yapping away to Donna, who was leaning against the counter.

"Hey, Jennifer," I said quietly as I walked over to her. I imitated Ray's quiet, snakelike anger. "What did you tell Suzanne about me?"

For a second she looked afraid, but then she snorted and went back to combing her hair.

"You better listen." I grabbed the hand that was doing the combing. "I left last night because I was sick! The two of you made me sick! Everything was fine with my customers. I don't want to have to pull all the hair off your head, so don't you ever lie about me again, you hear me?" I turned and strode toward the door. Before I left, I stopped and pointed at Donna. "And that goes for you too, Donna Lewis, and that feathered wig of yours." Before either of them could react, I pushed open the door and left.

I still had enough steam to carry me down the hall and knock on the office door. Suzanne opened it with a big smile, but when she saw it was me, her face got serious. "Come in, dear," she said.

I started to lose some of my nerve as I stepped into her office. "I think I need to clear something up," I said.

"I think you do," she said.

"I don't think you know the true reason why I left last night," I said. "I got sick."

"You were sick?"

"Yes, ma'am. I'd taken care of all my customers, and I asked Beth to pull my linens after the show."

Suzanne sat down at her desk, leaned back in her chair, and tapped her pencil against her sprayed hairdo. "I heard you left because you couldn't handle serving drinks."

I shook my head. "No ma'am. I left on account of feeling sick. I served my drinks all right."

"Well, you should have told me that you were leaving."

"I know. I made a mistake. I'm sorry."

She pointed her pencil at me. "You should always let someone in the office know if you're leaving."

"Yes ma'am."

"If you ever leave like that again without telling someone in charge, you'll lose your job."

I nodded. Just the possibility of ever being fired made me feel sick.

"You didn't have any trouble serving drinks?" she said.

"Not really. I was slow catching on, but I think it was fine in the end. At least everyone got what they'd ordered and I got their money."

"Okay." She sat forward in her chair and sighed. "Well, Tracy's going to be out for the rest of the week and probably next week too. She has mono or some dreadful thing. Can you keep covering for her?"

"Yes ma'am."

"Super." Suzanne stood up, then stopped like she'd just remembered something. She smiled and tilted her head. "Sunny, are you dating Joe Brady?" She sounded more like herself now and not like a boss.

I couldn't help smiling back at her. "No ma'am, we're not dating. I just tagged along with him and John Wells to the movies day before yesterday."

"Oh, my dear, that sounds delightful." She smiled back at me. You got the feeling that Suzanne was just crazy about men.

"Well, I better go set up," I said. "I have to ask Ross to show me some things." I backed toward the door. "I'm sorry about last night."

"Well, let's just forget it," she said. "Here, take your paycheck—"

"Thank you." I took my check from her, then I opened

the door and just about bumped into Joe Brady. "Oh!" I gasped.

"Hi, Sunny," he said.

"Hi." That was about all I could get out of my mouth; my heart was up around my ears.

"Joe, darling!" Suzanne said. "Your check's right here!" She handed him his check with a flourish. Then she winked at me. "I'll leave you two darlings alone. . . ." she said dramatically, and she sailed out of the office.

Joe stared after her with a puzzled look, then smiled at me. I sort of laughed.

"I didn't see you after the show last night," he said.

"Oh, I had to leave early because I got sick," I said. "But I'm fine now."

"Good." He kept staring at me. I had the funniest feeling he wanted to touch my hair.

"Well, I better get back to work. I'm serving drinks again tonight. I have to learn the different glasses."

"Okay," he said. Then, boy, if he didn't reach out and pat my hair!

"See you. . . ." I said.

He brushed his finger across my cheek real lightly. I just smiled like a fool, then opened the door and slipped out of the office. "Oh, wow," I breathed as I flew down the hall.

Donna and Jennifer were sitting at a table folding napkins. They ignored me, but who cared? I knew I had them beat by a mile now. I climbed the steps to my station and grabbed my water pitchers. On the way back down, my heart swooped and soared above the buffet tables. The food looked so beautiful—the roast beef and the banana salad and the little red cherry tomatoes—Joe Brady was really starting to fall for me, I could tell!

10

I didn't do too bad serving my drinks that night. The only mistake I made at the intermission was giving a woman a Tom Collins instead of the Jim Collins she'd ordered. But she didn't get mad. The fact that I was in good spirits and could joke about it helped; I told her I must have gotten my men mixed up.

As for Donna and Jennifer, I wasn't on speaking terms with the two of them anymore and that was fine with me. It did make my work load a whole lot heavier, though, because we used to be in the habit of helping each other out.

The next night I was still cleaning up my tables long after Donna and Jennifer had gone, and after most of the actors and actresses had left the theater too—all except John Wells and Joe. I was about to pull up my last tablecloth when I heard Joe Brady's laughter coming from the backstage area. I yanked so hard on my daggone cloth, I nearly wrapped myself up in it. A moment later Joe appeared with John. The two of them didn't seem to see me as they headed across the room. They were almost to the door when I croaked, "Hi there. . . ."

Joe looked up and I gave him a quick wave. He and John both waved back at me. I looked away and started folding up my cloth. I could hear them talking about me, but I couldn't make out what it was all about. "You're right," John said. "Ask her."

The next thing I knew, Joe was climbing the steps up to where I was.

"Sunny?" he said.

"What?"

"What are you doing now?"

"Well, I'm finishing up, but then I'm not doing anything."

"John and I want to know if you'll do us a favor."

"Sure, what is it?"

"We're going over to my apartment to read a new script a friend of mine in New York sent me. We want to put it on tape for her, and we need a girl about your age to read one of the parts."

"You do?" About fifty pounds of pressure started working on my inner ears.

"If you're not busy, you think you could come over for a couple of hours?"

"Sure." My head bobbed up and down like one of those plastic souvenir turtles. "Yeah, sure."

"Great. Do you need any help cleaning up?"

"No, just let me put these away," I said. I gathered up my load of dirty linens and started down the steps with Joe following me. "I'll just put these away," I repeated.

I hurried into the kitchen and dumped all my linens, then I pressed my hands against my hot forehead. You can do it, you can do it, I told myself. I stumbled over to the sink and drank some water—my throat was as dry as a bone. I tried to relax for a few seconds; then I walked stiffly back across the kitchen and pushed open the swinging door. "I have to stop long enough to call my folks," I said hoarsely.

"Sure," Joe said.

I walked with him and John down the hall and through the lobby without saying a word. I just kept directing my body to relax. When we got to the promenade, I excused myself and went to a pay phone. Larry answered. "Hey, it's me," I whispered. "Is Mama there?"

"Course she is. What's wrong?"

"Don't ask questions. Just put her on!"

"What happened—did you wreck your car?"

"*Larry*, put her on!" I whispered furiously.

"All right, hold your horses," he said.

I watched Joe and John as they pointed at some men's clothing in a shop window. Finally Mama came to the phone. I told her I was going out with a group from the theater and that I'd be home in a couple of hours. She acted a little hesitant till I started to get mad. I reminded her I was grown now, and that some people were married and had children at my age! She said okay, go on, but to be careful driving home.

I hung up and walked over to Joe and John. "All set?" Joe said.

"Yes."

"Good." He put his hand lightly against my back, and the three of us headed out of the mall.

"Listen, John, why don't you take my car?" Joe said when we got to the parking lot. "I'll ride with Sunny and show her the way."

Oh, Lord, he wanted to be alone with me in my car! I didn't know if my nerves could take it. Joe gave John his keys, then walked with me to my old Buick. Ray had found this old car in a junk lot and had fixed it up for my parents to give to me last Christmas.

"Turn onto the highway," Joe said. "The apartments are only about a mile from here."

I was so nervous I couldn't even look at him. I wished I'd seen him on his soap opera, so we'd at least have something to talk about. As I drove out of the parking lot, I cleared my throat, then said, "Did you enjoy working on a soap opera?"

"It was okay."

"I'm afraid I never saw it."

"You never saw it?" he said accusingly.

"No. . . ." I looked over at him. I couldn't tell if he was teasing me or not.

"I'm kidding," he said. "Actually it's a relief—I get tired of being recognized and answering questions about it all the time."

"You do?"

"Yeah."

"Oh. Well, I didn't recognize you at all!"

He laughed and so did I. Boy, he looked wonderful in the lights of the oncoming traffic. "Do you live near here?" he said.

"About ten miles away, in Wheeler."

"How big a town is Wheeler?"

"Oh, it's really not much more 'n just a wide spot in the road," I said.

He laughed again. "So do you know everyone in the town?"

"I guess I do. Between me and my family probably just about everyone."

"Is the rest of your family as sweet as you?"

I felt my face get warm. "No—they're sweeter," I said, joking.

"How sweet can they be?"

"Well, my parents are so sweet, they don't even yell at the dog!"

Joe laughed out loud, then looked out the front window. "It sounds like you have a nice life in Wheeler," he said.

"I guess I do, but I'd like to go to New York someday. I know there's nothing to compare with it."

"You don't need to go to New York. It's crazy up there."

"It is?" I stared at him while we were stopped at a light.

He nodded. "Yeah, it is. A lot of people suffer up there," he said.

"Like the people that don't have any place to live?"

"Yeah, and others."

The car behind me honked and we moved on. "How long have you lived up there?" I said.

"Two years."

"Did you go straight to New York when you left home?"

"Well, after I left college."

"Oh, you went to college?" I wondered just how old he was.

"Yeah."

"If you don't mind me asking—how old are you?" I said.

"I'm twenty-three. How old are you?"

"Eighteen."

"Really?"

"Yes, how old did you think I was?"

"Oh, I thought you were much older than me."

"You did?" This shocked me to death. "Most people think I'm younger than I am!"

"No," he said in a disbelieving way, but I could tell he was kidding now.

"Oh, quit that," I said, playfully slapping at him.

"I'm sorry," he said, laughing. "So, you're eighteen! Are you out of high school?"

"Of course I am—I graduated three weeks ago."

"Oh, congratulations."

"Thank you. I don't know if I'll make it to any college or not."

"Don't you want to go to college?"

"I don't think so. I'm not that smart, for one thing."

"You're not?"

"Well, I am in some ways, but not academic."

"Well, who cares about academic?" Joe said.

"The people who let you into college!" We laughed again. I was feeling good with him. Here I was just telling him the truth about myself, and he seemed to be getting a big kick out of it.

"Turn into that parking lot, Sunny," he said a moment later. He pointed at a huge apartment complex off the highway.

"Oh, is that where y'all live?"

"Yes."

"You live by yourself, or do you share a place with somebody?" I said.

"We each have our own apartment."

"Oh."

"Why? Are you looking for somebody to live with?" he said.

"Oh, no!" I could feel myself blush as we grinned at each other. I realized he was just kidding, but it gave me a thrill—the sexy way he'd said that.

11

"Okay, Sunny," Joe said. "You're playing Lilly. You're seventeen, and you live in Georgia with your father. John's your father." I smiled at John. We were sitting around a wooden coffee table in Joe's living room, and Joe was leaning forward and gesturing with his hands as he talked to us. "I'm a social worker who comes to your house. In the first scene, you're cleaning up and you hear a knock. Okay, ready to start?"

I frowned.

"What's wrong?"

"I'm not sure exactly what to do. I've never acted before."

Joe and John grinned at each other. "What is it you don't understand?" John said.

"Well, do I just wait my turn and read the lines, or what?"

"Yes, just read the lines under 'Lilly.' Don't read the sentences in parentheses—those are stage directions."

"The secret, sweetheart," John Wells said, "is to just be yourself. Pretend that this is your life. Don't act at all, okay? Just say the lines as if Sunny Dickens were saying them."

"Right, exactly," Joe said.

"Okay, I'll try," I said.

"Good, let's start." Joe clicked on his tape recorder, then sat back and rested his arm over the back of the sofa. He knocked on the wall. "Is anyone home?" he said.

"Who's there?" I said, reading the typed words in front of me.

"County Welfare Department," he said.

"Wait a minute. Yes?"

"Hi, my name's David Oglethorpe," Joe said. "Is your father here?"

"What do you want?" John Wells said in a sort of hillbilly voice. His accent tickled me.

After that Joe's and John's characters did most of the talking, but mine piped in now and then with a line. A couple of times the men seemed to get a kick out of the way I said something. I just sat there beaming through the whole first act. Who would have ever thought I'd be sitting in an apartment with two professional actors from

New York City reading a play with them? Not even my best dreams had been this good.

When we'd finished the first act, Joe clicked off his tape recorder. Then he sat back and rubbed his eyes with his fingers. "This is good," he said to John. "I think it's a pretty good script, don't you?"

"Not bad," John said.

Joe looked at me and smiled. "And you were very good," he said.

"Oh, I didn't do much," I said.

"No, but you were very good. You're a natural."

"Thank you."

"Would you like a beer?" he said.

"No, thank you."

"John? Beer?"

"Yeah."

Joe got up and went into the kitchen. John thumbed through the rest of the script, and I just looked around the room. There wasn't any decoration to speak of except for a couple of posters on the wall. One of them was all black with two yellow eyes. It said *Cats*. I got up and walked over to it, mostly for the excuse to stretch. When I turned around, I caught John Wells looking at me. "What's *Cats*?" I said.

"It's a musical that's running on Broadway," he said.

"Oh, was Joe in it?"

"No, his wife is in it."

"Oh." *His wife.* I turned back to the poster.

"Here we go," Joe said as he came back into the room with a couple of beers. I felt stunned as I walked back over to the sofa.

Joe picked up his script and said, "Okay, let's start." He turned on the tape recorder and settled back to read.

I had trouble reading my part this time; all my enthusiasm was gone. I couldn't believe I'd been so dumb—I'd never even imagined Joe Brady might be married—he didn't wear a ring. John Wells glanced at me a couple of times. I was afraid he was wondering why I was saying my lines so softly, so I tried to perk up.

When we were done reading, all I wanted to do was leave. The only trouble was I didn't know how to just get up and go without drawing a lot of attention to myself. I decided to wait for John Wells to go, and then leave with him. Finally, after he and Joe had discussed the play for a few minutes, he stood up and stretched. "Let's talk about this some more tomorrow," he said. "I'm pretty beat."

"Okay," Joe said.

I was starting to lean forward to get my pocketbook when I felt Joe's hand clamp down gently over mine. He didn't look at me; he just held my hand in place. My stomach took a giant dive and I kept still.

"You want to go to the gym tomorrow?" John asked Joe.

"Yeah, I'll meet you down at the car at ten."

"Okay," John said. He glanced at me. I wondered if he thought it was wrong for me to stay behind alone with

Joe. " 'Bye, Sunny, thanks for helping us out," he said.

"You're welcome."

After John left, Joe turned and looked at me. "Hi," he said.

"Hi," I said, then I pulled my hand out from under his and stood up. "I'm afraid I have to leave now."

I think I'd surprised him. "You have to leave now?" he said.

"Yes, I do."

"You can't stay for a little while?"

I shook my head. Actually I would have liked to fall into his arms then and there; my whole body was aching to go in that direction, but I fought against it. "No," I said.

He ran his fingers back through his hair as if I'd sort of thrown him for a loop; then he smiled and stood up. "Well, thanks for coming over," he said.

"You're welcome," I said as nicely as I could; I was afraid I might have hurt his feelings. I headed for the door and opened it. "See you later," I said.

He was just staring at me. " 'Bye, Sunny."

" 'Bye." I slipped out the door and nearly ran to the elevator.

Lying in my bed that night I felt tormented. I hugged my pillow, pretending that it was Joe, and at the same time I kept telling myself that I just had to forget him. I believed that being married meant you were bound to a particular person and you shouldn't fool around with anyone else. So if Joe Brady was interested in me, I felt like I should do everything in my power to resist him, even if it did make me miserable.

I was still going over my thoughts about marriage as I sat on our porch the next morning waiting for Larry. The two of us were going to the Goodwill store to deliver some things for my mother. "Watch it!" he said, coming out of the house with a box full of old winter clothes and games that we'd outgrown, like Chutes and Ladders and Go to the Head of the Class.

"Put it in my trunk," I said, following him to the car.

"It won't fit in your trunk, Sunny!"

"Okay, relax. The backseat then."

He positioned the box in the backseat. Then I gave him my car keys. I always let him back my car out of the driveway.

As I drove to town, I glanced over at Larry. "You ever think about getting married?" I asked him.

His mouth dropped open and he stared at me bug-eyed through his glasses.

"Don't look so stupid," I said.

"You getting married?"

"Of course not! I just wondered if you ever thought about it. For yourself."

"Well, who do you think I'm going to marry, Sunny?" he said, his voice cracking.

"I don't mean now. I mean in the future."

"Well, I don't know, Sunny," he said in an exasperated voice. "How could I know that?"

"This is not a test, Larry. I just wanted to have a conversation with you."

He laughed scornfully.

"What's wrong?" I said. "I'm not trying to put you on the spot! I just need someone to talk to."

"Well, talk to a girl," he said.

"Why, Larry? What's wrong with talking to you? That's what brothers are for. I'd like to have a man's point of view."

"Well, I don't have one." He turned and stared out the front window.

"What?"

"I don't have a man's point of view."

I looked over at him. My heart nearly broke. This was a hard time for him. He had pimples on his face and his body was getting longer and more gangly all the time, although his head didn't seem to be growing at all. He looked a little like a pinhead these days, I thought.

He caught me staring at him. "What's wrong?" he said belligerently.

"You've got a man's point of view. You're starting to look more like a man now."

He laughed cynically, but his face got red, I noticed.

"You are," I said. "You look good."

I'd gone too far. No one could believe that. He groaned like I made him sick, and he looked out his side window.

My mind was back on Joe Brady as I sat in the car waiting for Larry to come out of the Goodwill store. I wondered if Donna and Jennifer knew Joe was married. I bet the two of them wouldn't mind even if they did know. They probably got as much pleasure carrying on with married men as with single ones, I thought.

12

By the time the show was over that evening, I had decided to hurry out of the theater as fast as I could, so I wouldn't even be tempted to flirt with Joe Brady.

My plan got messed up, though, when he came out from backstage sooner than I'd expected. Before he saw me I stepped into the kitchen and peeked out the door. I watched him head over to Donna and Jennifer. They greeted him real boisterously; then I heard him say, "Is Sunny still here?"

I stopped breathing. Lord, I hadn't expected him to actually come looking for me!

"She must have left," Jennifer said.

Like heck. She knew good and well I hadn't left. Before I could stop myself, I stepped into the dining room.

"There you are," Joe said.

"Oh, hi," I said as if I was surprised to see him.

He grinned as he walked over to me. "I was looking for you."

"You were?"

"I was wondering if you'd like to go out for a little while tonight."

"Out?"

"Yeah."

I needed strength desperately—from somewhere I got a little. "No, I don't think I can," I said.

"Just for a little while? For a drink?"

I just stared at him.

"I'll get you home by bedtime," he said, smiling.

"All right," I breathed. A little drink wouldn't do any harm, I thought. Friends went and had drinks together. As long as we didn't get romantic. Though I didn't know if that was possible—my body felt like Jell-O as I headed out of the theater with him.

We drove to the Lone Spur Bar near Wheeler. It was dark and noisy when we entered the place. There was only one free stool at the bar—I sat on it while Joe stood beside me.

After he ordered us a couple of beers, we leaned against the bar and watched a country western band warm up to play. If it hadn't been for the fact that Joe was married, I know I would have inched over closer to him. I felt almost sick from wanting to kiss him and touch him, but I just sat there, drilling it into my brain that I was not going to let things go any further—or we'd both find ourselves in a lot of hot water.

After the band finished their set, Joe leaned over and whispered right into my ear, "Ready to go?" A chill went through me.

I nodded and got down off my stool. Just as we started to move through the crowd, I caught sight of Ray Perkins, of all people, sitting at the other end of the bar. He was looking right at me. I waved to him and he waved back, then turned his head and started talking with the woman who was sitting beside him. I couldn't tell if they were together or not, but she looked like she was thirty if she was a day.

Joe and I made our way through the crowd. Before we went out the door, I looked back to see Ray, but too many people were between us. I couldn't help feeling a little pleased that he'd seen me with Joe. Maybe now he'd get it into his head that I went out with grown men.

When Joe and I got into his car, he said, "Do you have to go home?"

"I guess I better."

We sat still for a moment, listening to the music starting up in the bar again. It was hard to make out Joe's face in the dark, but I could tell he was just staring at me. "You sure?" he said.

"Yes."

He put his car in gear and backed out of the parking

lot. I hoped he wasn't mad at me for being so standoffish. We didn't talk much as he drove me back to the mall so I could get my car. At one point he asked if I'd like to hear some kind of concertos and I said I would. He put a tape in his car's tape machine and wonderful sweet music started playing. It filled the car our whole ride back.

When we parked in the empty parking lot, Joe got out with me and walked me over to my Buick. Before I opened my door, I turned to him. "Well, thank you for the beers," I said. I started to turn away, but he took hold of my hand.

"Sunny . . . will you let me kiss you?" he said softly.

I lowered my head.

"C'mon, it won't hurt, I promise," he said in a sexy, teasing voice.

I laughed a little as I kept my head down. I wanted to kiss him more than anything in the world, but I was fighting it. I thought it was probably time to tell him how I felt about married men. "I can't," I said.

"Why not?"

I looked at him. "You're married, aren't you?" I said.

He didn't say anything for a moment, but he didn't let go of my hand either. If anything he squeezed it tighter. "You don't have to worry about that," he said.

"Why not?"

"You just don't."

"Wouldn't your wife mind if she knew you were kissing another girl?"

"I don't think so."

"How come?"

"She's with someone else these days. We're separated."

"Oh." I looked at him. "I'm sorry," I said.

"You're amazing," he whispered.

"Why?"

"I don't know many girls who would have stopped me because they thought I was married. You're very sweet, you know that?"

"No," I said in sort of a breathy voice.

"Yes," he said, and he put his hands around my bare arms and he squeezed me to him and he kissed me hard on the mouth. When he finished, he whispered in my ear, "You're wonderful."

I just held on to him. "Thank you," I said into his ear.

He moaned a little and hugged me tighter. After a moment, he gently pulled back from me and kissed my forehead. "Good night, honey," he said.

"Good night, Joe," I whispered.

He kept holding on to me with one hand as he opened my car door with the other. Then he sort of helped me down into the car. He touched my lips with his fingers before he moved away.

As I drove home, the moonlight shone in on my dashboard. The woods were bathed in blue light, and cool air blew through my window.

When I got into the house, it was dark except for the lamp in the hall. The dog barked from my parents' room and my mother called out, "Sunny?"

"Yes ma'am, I'm home."

I walked on air into my room and I slipped the bedspread off my bed. I carried it out to the front porch, and I sat down and wrapped it around me. I stared up at the moon and at the treetops and the stars. I felt like I was spinning with joy. I didn't have to worry about Joe's wife anymore. I went over his kisses and the pressure of his hands against my bare arms. I relived our whisperings to each other by putting my palm close to my mouth and whispering into it "Good night, honey." I remembered his little moan. I was trembling as I wrapped the bedspread tighter around me. Boy, it didn't seem like there was anything to stop us now.

13

I was still in heaven the next day. It was a beautiful Saturday. The humidity was real low, and it was cooler than it had been lately. Around noon I stepped lightly up the street to Ida Faye's house. She'd called me earlier to ask if I wanted to join her on a church picnic. I'd taken a long bath and dressed in a plaid sundress, and I felt more feminine than I had in a long time.

"Hey there!" I said when I got to her yard. Ida Faye was sitting on the porch dressed in a cherry-colored dress.

"You look real pretty," she said.

"That goes double for you."

"Thank you. Ray, we're ready," she called.

A moment later, Ray stood in the doorway.

"Hey," I said.

"Hey." He stared at me as he took a drag off his cigarette.

"How about us seeing each other last night?" I said.

He picked a piece of tobacco off his tongue. "Who was that you were with?"

"Joe Brady." I glanced at Ida Faye to see if his name had registered.

It had. "Oh, my word," she said.

"Who's he?" Ray asked her.

"He used to be Jimmy on *Another Love*," she said.

Ray looked back at me and I smiled at him. "Didn't he look like a soap opera star?" I said.

Ray shrugged.

"Where'd you go with him, Sunny?" Ida Faye asked.

"The Lone Spur—he took me there after the show."

"Isn't he a little old for you?" Ray said.

"No! He's about your age," I said. "But if you want to talk about old—what about that woman you were sitting with?"

That got him. He wasn't about to discuss his personal life with me and his grandmother. He just sort of chuckled and closed the door.

"Who was Ray with?" Ida Faye asked me.

"I don't know if he was actually with her or not," I said in a hushed voice. "But she looked real old."

"How old?"

"At least thirty."

Ida Faye laughed. "Ray, we better go now," she called.

"Is Ray coming with us to the picnic?" I said.

"No, he's just going to drive us over there," she said. "I tried to get him to come along, but he says he has work to do."

Ray came back out onto the porch, and he and Ida Faye and I climbed into his old station wagon. On the way to the picnic Ida Faye and I discussed her hairdo. She was planning on making an appointment to get another dye job. I told her she didn't need one, but she insisted that she did. Ida Faye was always concerned about her hair. Even now she pulled out a pink net to keep the wind from blowing it. "What price beauty?" she said as she tied the net under her chin. Ray and I looked at each other and laughed.

As we pulled up in front of the church, Ida Faye asked Ray if he wouldn't come on and join us. "Just for a little while?" she said.

"No, I don't think so," he said.

"Oh, come on," I said, boxing his arm.

"Oh, okay, but just for a little."

"Yay!" I said.

When we got out of the car, Ray offered to take Ida Faye's picnic basket, but she wouldn't let him. That's how she was. She seemed to know everyone in the world, too. I liked it when people said "Hi, Miss Ida Faye" to her.

The three of us headed over to one of the card tables that had been set up. In a meadow nearby a little Shetland pony was going around in circles carrying children on its back, and a band was playing some marching-type music. Ida Faye asked Ray if he'd help her start one of the grills. Ray said sure, and the two of them took off.

I sat at the table and squinted into the sunlight, watching the little pony. I was in the best mood. Everything seemed so alive and colorful—my flesh tingled with the memory of Joe hugging me. "Good night, honey" kept going through my head.

In a little while a clown came by and asked if I'd like to buy a pinwheel. I gave him fifty cents for one, and I carried it over to the cooking area. Ray looked up from poking at the coals on the grill and watched me as I floated up to him. I felt like he was admiring me in my dress. "I brought you a little present," I said, handing him the pinwheel.

"Hey, nice. Thank you. Hold it for me a second."

"No, I know, I'll stick it in your pocket," I said, and I put the pinwheel stick in Ray's back jeans pocket. Then I tapped the red plastic wheel to make it spin. "This can be your little motor," I said.

"Motor for what?" he said.

"Whatever you want." I smiled knowingly at him, then I went over to Ida Faye. She introduced me to a couple of young men she was talking to. I thought they looked at me like they thought I was attractive too—dang, I felt like I was appealing to the whole world today, as if everyone sensed that a TV star had fallen for me!

After we ate some hot dogs, Ray told Ida Faye he was taking off to pick up some car parts, but he'd return shortly to get us. She told him not to worry about coming back, that somebody would give us a ride home.

"I don't mind," Ray said.

"No, no, honey, it's not necessary," Ida Faye said.

Ray just stood there, hesitating. He was looking at me as if he wanted me to go with him or something. Boy, when it rained, it poured! Just a week ago I'd have done anything to get Ray's attention, but it didn't affect me that much right now with Joe Brady so much on my mind.

"Well, 'bye," he said abruptly.

" 'Bye," I said, waving. "Catch you later."

I thought I looked especially good getting ready to go to work that night. I'd gotten some sun on my face at the picnic, and my hair seemed better than usual. What in the world was going to happen with me and Joe Brady to-night? I wondered. Would we kiss again, and if we did, would we go beyond that? I bathed, then I selected my underwear as carefully as if I was a bride. I had to laugh —about the only thing I could really be sure of happening tonight was getting hot and sweaty from serving drinks, but it gave me a thrill to behave as if I was dressing for Joe. Believe me, I'd never gotten this kind of thrill when I'd prepared for my dates with Buddy Willis.

I was so excited clearing my tables that night that my hands were trembling. When I caught sight of Joe, I turned away and pretended to be concentrating real hard on folding up a tablecloth. I didn't look at him as he climbed the steps to where I was.

"Hi," he said.

"Hey." I smiled at him, but I didn't move toward him. I just kept folding my tablecloth. He sat down at the table nearest me and leaned his cheek against his hand as he watched me. His pose reminded me of a Marlon Brando poster Debbie used to have.

"What did you do today?" he said after a moment.

"I went to a church picnic."

"A church picnic? What kind of church?"

"Baptist."

"Really? Is everyone there real conservative?"

"I don't think so—it's not that strict," I said.

"What was it like?"

"It was nice."

"Was there music?"

"Just a little homemade band."

"That sounds nice. What else did they have?"

"A pony ride for the kids, and hot dogs."

He was staring right at me. His eyes seemed to be twinkling. "What else?" he said.

I just stared back at him and grinned. He reached out suddenly and took my hand and pulled me over to him. "What else was at the picnic?" He tugged on my hand, forcing me to sit down in the chair beside him.

"A clown selling pinwheels."

"What else?" His face was real close to mine.

"Nothing. . . ." I felt short of breath.

"Nothing?"

"You're making me nervous," I whispered.

"Oh, yeah?" He leaned over and kissed my lips lightly, and then he looked at me. "Stay like this," he said.

"Like what?"

He touched the collar of my blouse and then my chin. "Sweet and lovely . . . I have to go to some dumb thing given by one of the theater patrons tonight, so stay like this until tomorrow, okay?"

"Okay."

He stared at me for a moment, then stood up and headed gracefully down the stairs and out of the theater. It was a moment before I could breathe normal again. He'd just about wiped me out.

14

I don't know how I lived till the Sunday matinee. I thought about Joe all night and the next morning. When I got to the theater I was beside myself, anticipating him around every corner. I couldn't even take a drink at the water fountain without thinking that he might come up behind me and grab me or something.

The funny thing is that when he did appear I was least expecting it. I was making coffee and fantasizing about what it would be like to be his wife. I was picturing us living up in New York and coming back to Wheeler now and then and bringing presents for everyone. I was thinking that I'd like to give Ida Faye a video recorder for her

TV so she could record one soap on her bedroom TV while she watched another one in the living room. Suddenly Joe Brady said, "Hi, angel."

"Oh!" I nearly jumped out of my skin.

"I'm sorry," he said, putting his hand on my arm. "Did I scare you?"

I laughed and nodded. I was also embarrassed, being as how I'd just been imagining us married.

He touched my hair. "Will you have dinner with me between shows?"

"Yes."

"Wait for me."

"Okay."

He pinched my cheek lightly, then took off.

When the matinee was over, I waited for him near the door that led to the backstage area. On his way out, some autograph seekers waylaid him. One man asked him for a picture to give to his girlfriend. Joe gave him one, and the man said, "Hot damn—maybe with this I'll get lucky tonight!"

Next a couple of overweight girls asked Joe to autograph their programs. After he did, they shook hands with him. As they passed by me, I heard one of them say, "My heart's beating so fast!"

"So's mine," the other said, "and my hand was all sweaty!"

"Oh, no!"

"Yes!"

I smiled at them, sort of wishing they knew I was Joe's date. But he didn't come over to me until after everyone was gone. "Hey you—d'you want my autograph?" he said.

"Heck, no, I don't even know who you are," I said.

He laughed and put his hand against the wall, penning me in close to him. "Oh, you don't, huh? Where do you want to go?"

"I don't care. Any place's fine."

"How about my place?"

Boy, this took me by surprise. "Do we have time?" I said, trying to sound nonchalant. "I have to be back here to set up in about an hour."

"Then we don't have time. But we'll have plenty of time after the show tonight." He tipped his head down to mine so that our foreheads were barely touching. "What do you say?"

"About what?"

"You want to come over to my place after the show?"

I didn't say anything. Of course I wanted to go, but I was a little scared too. Being alone with him in his apartment would probably mean just one thing.

"Hmm?" he said.

I nodded.

"Good," he said. Then he put his arm around my shoulders and we started out of the theater.

We went to a little restaurant called the Bavarian Cafe. It was made up to look like a restaurant in Germany with big sausages hanging overhead. We sat at a candlelit table in the back. I had no idea what my food tasted like—I wasn't paying a bit of attention to my salami sandwich. I just remember Joe's handsome face glowing in the candle-light. After the meal his legs went around one of mine under the table and he gave it a squeeze. My stomach took one of those giant dives. "Ready to go?" he said.

"Yes."

We got up and he paid the bill at the register; then we headed on back to the theater.

Just before the play started, I placed a call home. Larry answered and said that Mom and Dad had gone to an Auxiliary dinner. I told him to tell them that I was going out with some of the actors from the theater after the show, and then to cover my bases I added that if we stayed out real late, I was going to sleep over with the girl who played Laura in the play. After I hung up, I felt relieved—I was glad my parents had been out, so I hadn't had to lie to them directly.

During the evening show my eyes were glued to Joe up on the stage. The whole time he was talking and moving, all I could think about was the lean, graceful body under his clothes and the mystery of it, and that in just a few hours the two of us would be alone together in his apartment. After the show I stood by the backstage door, waiting for him. When he came out, he was talking to John. He just put his arm around me and he kept talking to John as the three of us headed out of the theater. I loved the way he was acting so casual—you'd have thought we went home together every night. When we got out to the parking lot, he said good night to John, then he suggested that I follow him home in my car.

He was waiting for me when I pulled into his parking lot a few minutes later. He slipped his hand around mine when I got out of my car, and without saying anything, we walked into his building and got into the elevator.

I was tongue-tied by the time we entered his apartment —from pure excitement and from fear too. He got a couple of beers out of the fridge. Then we sat down next to each other on his couch. He was keeping his eyes on me, but I was finding it hard to look at him. In fact, I was wishing we could turn on the TV or something, anything to diffuse some of the excitement I was feeling. I took a sip of beer and said, "Did the TV come with the apartment, or is it yours?"

He stared at me with a little smile. "It's mine—I brought it from New York."

"Oh. It's nice," I said, just staring at the blank set, then I had to laugh. What in the world was I saying?

He laughed too. It was like we were both on the same wavelength about what was going on—here we were in his apartment all alone after days of flirting and carrying on with one another....

He reached out and took my beer can out of my hand. As he put it on the coffee table, I looked down at the floor. He gently turned my face toward him. "Does it scare you to be alone with me?" he said.

"Yes," I said.

He put his arm around me and pulled me over to him a little. "I won't hurt you," he said.

"I know."

"Will you stay all night?"

I just sat very still. I wanted to stay, but I didn't know how to tell him that I was a virgin and that I didn't take birth control pills or anything like that.

"Will you?" he said into my hair.

"Stay?" I said.

"Yes."

I could hardly talk. I knew I should talk to him about those things now, but it embarrassed me. "Well, I've never—" I stopped right there.

"What?" he said. "Never what?"

"Slept with anyone," I whispered. My eyes were closed; this was so hard to talk about.

"Really? Gee, I don't know if I've ever known a virgin before. . . ."

"Ohh—" I started to pull away from him.

"I'm sorry," he said, grabbing me back. "I was kidding. Hey—" He took hold of my hand. "I think that's wonderful, really. What I meant to say is that I've never known a girl like you before. You seem so pure."

I wasn't pure, but if he liked to think that, I didn't think I should contradict him.

"Listen, we don't have to do anything. We can just lie down together and go to sleep—how's that?" he said.

I didn't think we had to be that extreme, but I just nodded and whispered, "Okay."

"Good. Come on, let's go into my room."

I stood up with him and we sort of held our arms around each other as we went back to his dark bedroom. He turned on his bedside lamp and said, "I'll be right back."

He went into the bathroom and a moment later came out. He unbuttoned his shirt as he walked toward me. I wondered if I should take off my T-shirt now or what. Actually I wouldn't have minded taking off all my clothes.

He sat down beside me and rested his hand against my back. "You can sleep in your clothes if you want to," he said.

"Well, I guess I don't mind taking some things off," I said hoarsely.

"Fine." He stood up and undid his jeans. As he slipped out of them, I took off my shoes, then I unzipped my slacks. After I pulled them off, we sat side by side on the bed. I didn't look down at his underwear; considering how things were going, it would have seemed rude, I thought.

"Let's get in bed," he said softly. I stood up as he pulled the bedspread and sheet back, then we lay down together.

He put his arm under my head and pulled me close to him. I turned sideways and put my hand on his bare chest. His chest hairs felt dry and soft. He reached out with his free hand and switched off the light. I was still as a statue while he gently patted my head. I wondered if we were really just going to sleep—or would we at least kiss and do something.

"Good night," he said after a moment. He kissed the top of my head, then grew still.

I didn't close my eyes. I listened to the traffic sounds coming from the highway and to the sound of Joe Brady's breathing. I could feel his heart beating under my hand.

15

It was hot. I opened my eyes. The sun was streaming in the window, showing little particles of dust dancing above us. Joe's arm was still around me and my hand was on his chest. He seemed to be sleeping. I eased myself up off the bed and went into the bathroom. I used the toilet, splashed water on my face, then combed my hair with my fingers and ate a little daub of toothpaste.

I walked back to the bed and lay down next to Joe. He had rolled over onto his side while I was in the bathroom, and now his back was to me. I closed my eyes, but there was no way I was going to sleep. If I hadn't slept all night, I wasn't about to start now.

I was lying on my side just killing time when I felt the mattress sink in. Joe was turning over. I felt his breath against the back of my neck. I got goose bumps. He put his hand on my arm, and suddenly without thinking I turned over and melted right into him, burying my face against his naked shoulder. He clutched my arms and I moved my hips against his. He was hard. I kissed his warm neck, then I kissed him on the mouth and pressed myself harder against him. Just as I was starting to wrap my bare legs around his, he let go of my arms and pulled away. "No," he breathed. He rolled over onto his back and closed his eyes and took a deep breath.

I was bewildered—what in the world had just happened? I touched his arm. He opened his eyes and looked at me. "We can't, Sunny," he said.

"Why not?"

"I don't want to take advantage of you."

"Why?"

"You're too nice."

"No, I'm not," I said. I wasn't—I *wanted* us to make love now.

He picked up his pillow and playfully put it over my face.

"I'm not," I said again in a muffled voice.

But he seemed to be ignoring what I was saying. He lifted the pillow and quickly kissed my forehead, then picked up his watch from the bedside table. "It's almost ten," he said. "You want to have a breakfast special with me at the mall?"

I barely nodded—I felt very frustrated.

"Good," he said. "Let me hop in the shower first." He gently unwound himself from me, then got up and went into the bathroom.

When the door closed, I sat up and picked my slacks up off the floor. I couldn't figure out why Joe had changed his mind so quickly just now. Had he gotten turned off when he'd remembered I was a virgin? Couldn't he tell I was over being scared? Last night I'd sort of let my nervousness get the best of me, but this morning I'd felt more free about expressing myself.

A moment later he came out of the bathroom. He had a blue towel wrapped around his waist. He walked to his dresser and started rummaging around in a drawer. I figured he might like some privacy to dress. "Are you through in the bathroom?" I said.

"Sure, go ahead."

While I was showering, I was wondering if I should try and talk with him about what had just happened. I wanted to tell him he shouldn't worry about taking advantage of me or anything—I was able to decide for myself whether or not I wanted to make love with him. But when I stepped back into the room and saw him sitting there all dressed and waiting for me, I felt too inhibited to say anything.

"Ready?" he said.

I nodded.

"Let's go, then." Without touching me, he led the way out of his room.

*　　*　　*　　*　　*

We went to the Fancy Coffee Shop at the mall. That was just the name of the place—it wasn't all that fancy. We had the breakfast special for just a dollar fifty each. I didn't talk much. Besides being worn out from not sleeping all night, I was starting to feel self-conscious. Things seemed different with Joe now. He didn't really flirt with me, for one thing. In fact, he read *The New York Times* the whole time he ate. He gave me a section of it to look at, but it didn't interest me at all. I was just thinking about the two of us and wondering what was going on in his mind.

When the waitress finally took our plates away, he folded up his paper. He sipped his coffee, then looked at me. "What are some of your interests, Sunny?" he said.

That took me by surprise. "Well, I like to play the guitar," I said.

"Oh, yeah? What kind of songs do you like to play?"

"Do you know a song called 'Mamas, Don't Let Your Babies Grow Up to Be Cowboys'?" I wasn't totally lying —I figured I'd get Ray to teach me that song real soon.

He laughed. "I don't know it—it sounds great."

"It is great," I said, pleased that I'd made him laugh.

"Do you like to read?" Joe said.

"No, I'm afraid I don't read much."

"How come?"

"I guess I never got the habit," I said. I thought this comment would tickle him too, but he didn't seem to be that amused; in fact, his look made me wish I'd told him I did like to read. "I do like to read some things," I said.

"Like what?"

"Well, my neighbor just lent me some astrology books. Do you believe in astrology?"

"No, not really."

"I guess I don't really, either." I could feel my face growing red. "Do you like to read?" I asked him.

He nodded again; then his eyes wandered around the room and he made a writing motion in the air. He must be asking for the check, I thought, looking over my shoulder. This was terrible—it was obvious he was bored with me. "What do you like to read?" I said, looking back at him.

"Oh. Lots of things."

The waitress gave Joe the check. "Let's go," he said. He put some money on the table and we got up to leave.

Outside the hot air smelled like tar as we started across the parking lot. I wondered if he planned to just take me back to my car now or what. I hated leaving him when things were going so badly.

When we got in his car, he looked over at me. "Want to stay with me a little longer?" he said.

"Yes," I said.

"Do you know any good places to go?"

"Um, well, what kind of places?"

"Oh, a park or something."

"I do know of one little park. It just has a playground and a little zoo—"

"That sounds nice," he said.

"It is nice." I felt proud of myself for remembering

Lyman Park—I thought sure Joe would like it since he loved children's things so much.

He started up his car, then put that concerto tape in his tape machine. As we rode out to the park, the dramatic violin music made everything we passed seem so beautiful. I loved being with Joe—it was like being in a movie.

When we got to the park, it was pretty deserted. I guessed this was an odd time for grown people to be out playing —eleven A.M. on a Monday morning. We got out of the car and started across a grassy meadow together. The sky was clear and pine trees made shadows at the edge of the meadow.

Out of the blue Joe took my hand. I felt such a surge of joy that I gave his hand a tug, and before you knew it we were running. We ran about a hundred yards before we stumbled to a halt under the trees, winded and laughing. "You're fast," Joe said, breathing hard. He was still holding my hand.

"Running's one of the things I do best," I panted.

"Oh, it is?" he said, ruffling my hair.

"Yes, it is," I said, giggling.

We began walking together through the little pine woods toward the zoo cages. When we got to the zoo, we found one monkey in a cage and a pair of spindly goats in another one. The monkey was pacing around his cage with wild eyes.

"He's pitiful," I said, meaning the monkey.

"Yeah, he is," Joe said. "This is disgusting."

"It really is! I had no idea!" I said. I felt worried that he might think less of me since I'd suggested we come here. "Let's go to the swings," I said quickly. "Come on." I charged over to the swing area, anxious to get us away from the shabby cages. I jumped on one of the swings and started pumping my legs hard and letting my head fall back.

Joe came over to the swings and sat on one that was two swings away from me—even a dumb little thing like that could make me worry. I pumped my legs harder and swung higher.

Joe just swayed gently on his swing, keeping his feet on the ground as he looked off into the distance. I felt like an idiot for swinging so high, so I slowed down till I was moving as slow as him.

"This is peaceful," he said after a moment.

"It is. It's like playing hookey from school," I said.

He smiled and nodded.

We both just rocked in unison for a while as the warm wind shook the tree leaves. The air was sweet smelling, and you could hear the sound of trucks going down the highway. I was dying to tell him that I liked being here with him, that I liked staying over with him last night, and that he shouldn't worry about me being so pure. But before I could even begin to think of how to say these things, he stood up and started walking away. I watched him, not knowing if I was supposed to follow or not.

After he'd gone a little ways, he looked back at me. "Coming?" he said. He looked beautiful standing there in the sunlight with his dark hair shining. My legs felt wobbly as I stood up and went to him.

When we stepped out into the sunny meadow, he stopped and knelt down in the tall dusty grass. He unbuttoned his shirt, then lay back with his eyes closed. His chest hairs glistened in the light.

I sat near him and self-consciously picked some wild daisies from the grass.

After a couple of minutes he reached out for me, and he pulled me down so that my head was lying on his bare chest. His skin smelled salty with sweat and his chest hairs tickled my nose. I was real happy to be this close to him, but I was also uncomfortable. It was sweltering lying there right under the hot sun. Insects were landing on me and my nose itched like crazy, but I didn't scratch or squirm. I tried to stay still by keeping my eyes closed and imagining that me and Joe Brady were melting into the sun. After a few minutes he sat up and patted me on the back. "It's hot," he said. "Let's go."

When we pulled into the parking lot of his building, he parked next to my Buick. He cut off his engine and pulled out the tape of concertos—we'd listened to them on the ride home too, but this time, instead of making everything seem beautiful, they'd only added to the anxiety I felt about leaving him.

He looked at me and picked a piece of grass out of my hair. "Thank you for your company," he said.

"Thank you for yours," I said.

He turned away and opened his car door. I got out and followed him over to my car. He held my door open and watched me slip down into the driver's seat without kissing me or anything. "I'll talk to you later, okay?" he said.

I wanted to ask him when was *later,* but I just smiled artificially and said, "Okay."

"Good-bye, Sunny."

" 'Bye, Joe."

He waved at me, then took off for his apartment. The wind was blowing a little, causing his yellow shirttails to flap out behind him like butterfly wings.

16

I felt upset driving home. What had Joe meant by *later*? The theater was closed tonight since it was Monday, so did he mean he'd see me tomorrow night after the show— or did he mean he'd call me later and arrange to see me before then? Thinking back over the last twelve hours, I was afraid I might have wrecked everything when I'd acted so timid last night. Why hadn't I just gone to bed with him and let him discover for himself I was a virgin? By then it would have been too late for him to change his mind.

As I drove into our driveway, the door off the kitchen opened and my dad stepped out to the carport. I was surprised to see him. He never came home for lunch. I got out of my car and waved at him, but he didn't wave back.

"Hi," I said. "What are you doing here?"

"Waiting for you. Where have you been?"

"Didn't Larry tell y'all? I stayed over with the girl who plays Laura in the play."

"Well, we know that you didn't do that," he said.

I just stared at him.

He opened the door off the kitchen. "Let's go in," he said.

I went into the house, and he followed me through the kitchen. I started to head back to my room, because I wasn't sure what else to do. I was too tired to think really straight.

"Sunny—"

"What?"

"Stay in here," he said.

I sat down on the sofa in the family room and stared at the floor. Dad didn't sit. "You want to tell me where you've been?" he said.

"What makes you think I didn't stay over with that actress?" I said.

"Because I called the theater this morning and got her number and called her."

"Oh, no! You didn't! Oh, that embarrasses me to death! What'd she say?"

"She didn't even know who you were."

My stomach curled up. "Oh, why did you call her?" I yelled.

"You didn't answer my question."

"What question?"

"Where were you?"

"I was with a friend! But we didn't do anything, I promise!" I got up and crossed the room. This was mortifying—I'd never discussed these kinds of things with my father.

"Who is he?" he said.

"What do you want to know for? So you can call him too? You had no right calling that actress, Daddy!"

"What's his name?" he asked quietly.

"Joe Brady!" I yelled. "But I'm telling you the truth—he didn't bother me or anything. I swear it!"

My dad stared at me for a long moment; his eyes looked sort of watery. I turned away from him and sat down on the couch. Suddenly he started into the hallway. "Where you going?" I shrieked.

He didn't answer me. I heard him pick up the phone. "Don't!" I shot into the hall like a ball of fire and yanked the receiver from him. *"Don't you dare call him!"*

He stared at me like I'd lost my mind. "I'm calling Mother to tell her you're home," he said in a strange voice.

I could have died. "Oh." I handed him back the receiver. "Well, I'm sorry, I didn't know who you were calling." While he dialed, I went back to my room and sat on my bed and put my head in my hands. It was making me sick that this was happening.

A moment later I heard Daddy hang up the phone. I

heard him moving around the kitchen, then the screen door slammed, and his car motor started up. Tears came to my eyes—he hadn't even said good-bye.

I napped nightmarishly for a while. When I woke up, I heard my mother in the kitchen. I got up and went in there, but she didn't look at me as she took glasses out of the dishwasher.

"Are you giving me the cold shoulder?" I said.

"Not necessarily," she said, but she still didn't look at me.

"Did you talk to Daddy?" I said.

"Yes."

"What'd he say?"

"He thinks you've flipped."

"Flipped! Oh, I have *not* flipped! Now—now why does he think that—I have not fl—" Suddenly I broke down crying. It was the combination of everything I guess—not getting enough sleep, worrying about Joe, fighting with my dad. I sobbed as I headed back to my room.

My mother followed me and stood in my doorway as I wept loudly on the bed. "Don't cry, honey," she said.

"Y'all have really upset me!" I said.

She walked over to the bed and sat down next to me. "But you lied about where you were going, Sunny."

"But if I'd told you the truth, you wouldn't have let me go, would you?" I said. "I'm tired of being treated like a tiny child! Lots of girls my age live by themselves—or they're married already and have two or three children!"

"You're exaggerating," Mama said.

"I am not," I sobbed.

"We just don't want this man to take advantage of you and hurt your feelings."

"He won't! He thinks like y'all do! He's more old-fashioned than you'd ever believe!"

"He's a lot older than you from what I gather."

"But he's so nice. He's—he's everything a woman could dream of!" I started crying again. Everything at the moment was breaking my heart.

When I wiped my eyes and looked up, I saw my dad standing in the doorway. I hadn't heard him come in the house. I couldn't tell what he was feeling—he was such a poker-faced type of person when emotional things were going on.

My mother handed me a tissue. "Here—we're not mad at you," she said.

"Daddy is," I said.

"Daddy's not mad," she said.

I blew my nose. "He didn't say good-bye." It still upset me he hadn't said good-bye earlier—sometimes a little thing like that can destroy you.

"Are you mad?" Mama asked him.

He barely shook his head.

"He just cares about you," my mother said. "He doesn't want you to get hurt."

"I blame him," Dad said simply.

"For what?" I cried. "We lost track of the time, so I asked if I could sleep over because I was scared to drive home so late! He didn't take advantage of me or anything!"

"I think he should have driven you home if it was too late for you to drive."

"Well, it's *my* fault that he didn't!" I lied. "He offered to, but I didn't want to put him to the trouble!"

"I guess you can't blame him then," Mama said to Dad. I could tell she was just trying to bring back peace between us all.

My dad came over to the bed and sat down. "Well, okay," he said, sighing. "Let's forget it."

At that moment Larry peeked into my room. He must have been unnerved to see the three of us just sitting there in a row, because he sort of laughed like a hyena and disappeared.

"This place is a nuthouse," I said, sniffing.

Mama and Daddy smiled. They were starting to act more like themselves again.

Every time the phone rang that evening, I jumped up from the couch and charged out to the hall to grab it. But it was always for Larry. The fourth time it was for him, I said, "It's for you, you idiot—hurry up and get off!"

Larry brushed me aside, but my mother seemed disturbed by my fury. As I sat back in front of the TV, I caught her looking at me with a worried expression. "Sunny, what are you so anxious about the phone for?" she said.

"I'm not anxious!" I said, near tears.

"Are you expecting a call from someone?" she said. I knew she knew it was Joe.

"No, no one in particular."

She went back to minding her own business, and I just kept staring blindly at the TV all evening, waiting for him to call.

17

The next morning I hung around waiting for the phone to ring till finally its silence got to be so upsetting that I banged out of the house and went up the street to visit with Ray and Ida Faye.

I managed to calm down quite a bit visiting with Ida Faye. I especially got a kick out of watching *The Price Is Right* with her—she'd try real hard to guess all the prices. The two of us sat in her living room in front of the TV while a big floor fan blew warm air over us. I actually preferred a fan to air conditioning—with a fan you could keep the doors and windows open and feel more connected to the outside world.

Ray was out in the yard all morning working on a car. Once he passed through the living room and said, "Hey, girls."

"Hey," Ida Faye and I answered. When he passed back through the room, I said, "Take a break."

"In a minute."

But it was over an hour before he appeared again. He came back into the house and announced he was hungry.

"I'm hungry too. Are you, Sunny?" Ida Faye said.

"Yes ma'am."

"Well, let's all go back in the kitchen," she said.

Ray and I followed her down the hall. We sat at the white enamel kitchen table while Ida Faye peered in the refrigerator. I loved her kitchen. It had big windows, and the floor was real old with faded pink and green tiles.

"Well, here's some deviled eggs to get you started," she said, and she put a plate of eggs on the table. Then she started bringing out a bunch of other dishes left over from the big Sunday dinner she'd cooked. "I'll heat up these greens and this cornbread," she said. "Here's some slaw and butter beans and ham and biscuits. Let's see . . . I've got a good tomato here. . . . You reckon that'll be enough?"

Ray and I cracked up. "No," I said, "I'm going home," and I pretended to get up in a huff.

"Sorry, Grandma," Ray said like he was going to leave with me.

"Oh, you two." She smiled at us. "What I mean is, I don't have any more stew meat."

"I think we'll forgive you," Ray said. "It all looks pretty good to me. You're something. You know that?"

"You sure are," I said.

"Y'all want some iced tea?" she said, ignoring our praise.

Once we sat down, she asked Ray if he'd fixed the car he was working on all morning.

"Oh, yeah," he said. "I got it running like a little sewing machine."

"Ha!" I laughed.

"What was the matter with it?" Ida Faye asked.

Ray went on to talk about filters and pumps; it didn't make a bit of sense to me. "Hey—how'd you learn so much about cars?" I said.

"Just picked it up," he said.

"Ray's smart like that," Ida Faye said. "He can learn anything. He'll thoroughly deny it, but it's true."

"Oh, you really think Ray's smart?" I said teasingly.

"I think he's a genius," Ida Faye said.

Ray and I laughed.

"No, seriously," she said. "When he was little, he'd just sit there taking everything in, not talking much. You didn't realize he was even paying attention till he'd come out with some real intelligent remark that showed he knew everything that was going on."

"So he didn't talk much even when he was little?" I said.

"No, he didn't. Did you now?" she asked him.

"I guess not," he said like he was amused at us talking about him.

"But you—now *you* couldn't be topped when it came to talking," Ida Faye said to me.

"She sure couldn't," Ray said, shaking his head.

"I've heard this before," I said.

"When Larry was just born, your mother'd send you up here and you'd follow everybody around and talk on and on like a little bird, remember, Ray?"

"Sure—I used to hide from her," Ray said.

"I remember that," Ida Faye said. "She'd march through the house calling, 'Ray! Ray!' and you'd be in the closet—"

"That was cruel!" I said.

"Oh, but he loved you, honey, didn't you, Ray? Tell the truth."

"Yeah, I guess I did. She was pretty cute."

"Oh, she was. She was real cute," Ida Faye said.

"That's enough about me, y'all. I can't take any more," I said.

"Here, Ray, finish these biscuits," Ida Faye said, handing him the plate of biscuits.

"No ma'am—it'll kill me," he said.

"Put a good piece of tomato on it, here."

"Oh, okay."

After we finished, we all sat for a while back in the living room with the fan blowing on us. Ida Faye closed her eyes and napped, even though she continued sitting straight up in her chair.

Ray and I got a big kick out of watching *People's Court*. I wished Ida Faye wasn't missing it. She always liked to voice her opinion on who should win. On this particular day both parties were so stupid, I couldn't imagine who she would have picked.

After a while Ray went back to work outside. Ida Faye woke up, and we watched *Andy of Mayberry* together. Finally I dragged myself up and said I had to go home and vacuum—I'd promised I'd do that for my mother before I went to work.

I said good-bye to Ida Faye and thanked her for the good lunch, then headed across the yard. "See you later," I called to Ray.

"Where you going?"

"Home to vacuum."

He waved at me and I waved back. Walking down the hill, I still felt peaceful from having been with those two. But as soon as I entered our yard, I began to go to pieces —my heart raced and my stomach started feeling sick. I went in the house and casually asked if there'd been any calls for me.

"Nah," Larry said as he watched the TV. It wasn't his fault, but I just hated him in that moment.

I went back to my room and threw myself down on my bed. I didn't have the energy anymore to vacuum.

18

I was getting ready for work when the phone finally rang. I charged out to the hall, but Larry got it before me.

"It's for you," he said.

"Is it a man?" I mouthed.

"Yeah," he mouthed back, and he winked at me.

I think I loved Larry in that moment as much as I'd hated him earlier. I was breathless as I took the phone from him. "Hello," I said into the receiver.

"Hey there."

I was confused to hear Ray's voice. "Ray?"

"Yeah."

"Oh. Hi."

"I meant to ask you something earlier."

"What?"

"What are you doing tonight?"

"I have to work."

"I mean after work."

"Oh, I have a date," I said. At least I was praying I'd have a date with Joe.

"Oh . . . okay."

"Why?" I said.

"I just wanted to know if you'd like to go hear some music."

"Hear music where?"

"At the Tin Can over in Taylorsville. An old friend of mine's playing there."

"Oh, darn—I'd love to go there! I've always wanted to go there!"

"Well, maybe some other time."

"Oh, you'll forget."

"No, I won't. Well, don't do anything I wouldn't do."

I sighed with despair. I really wasn't in the mood to joke now. "Okay, I'll see you later," I said.

" 'Bye," he said, and he hung up.

Now just watch it take Ray Perkins another eighteen years before he asks me out again, I thought.

I had no idea what would happen after the show that night. Were Joe and I a couple now? Or just friends, or what? It seemed to me we'd gone a lot further than just two friends, being as how we'd slept together in our underwear and had breakfast at the mall and gone to the park together. As I went about my work, I kept going over all the evidence that proved we were more than just friends.

But at the end of the evening Joe didn't come out from the backstage area. I knew he had to go through the theater to leave, because the back door got locked real early; but long after the others had cleared out, he still hadn't appeared. I felt sick as I wiped down the coffee machine for the tenth time, thinking that if he'd really wanted to see me, he'd have come out by now.

My heart jumped when I heard footsteps—I turned my head—but it was just the stage manager. I was shaking after he left. Damn! I thought, throwing down my cleaning rag. This was making me so mad! I brushed the tears from my eyes and glared at the stage door. I hated myself for acting like such a wimp. That's what had wrecked things between me and Joe to begin with, I thought—when I'd acted so scared in his living room the other night. It wasn't like me to act that way! My whole life till now I'd been forward and outgoing with the opposite sex.

I grabbed my pocketbook, marched down the steps, and opened the door that led backstage. I'd never been backstage before. As I moved through a dark area filled with folding chairs and clothing racks, I heard voices coming from a room at the end of a hallway.

I went down the hall and stopped outside the room. Joe and John were talking. "Joe?" I said. I had no idea what I would say when he came out—just pure nerve had brought me this far.

"What was that?" John Wells said.

"What?" Joe said.

"Joe?" I said louder.

I heard a chair move; then Joe stepped into the shadowy hallway.

"Hi," I said.

"Oh, hi, Sunny," he said.

I couldn't tell if he was glad to see me or not. I wracked my brain to come up with some excuse for tracking him down. "I just came back to ask you something," I said.

"What?"

"Well, I was wondering if you had plans for the Fourth of July." I could have died, I could have died, I felt so stupid!

"The Fourth of July? No, not as far as I know. When is it—day after tomorrow?"

"Yes."

"Why?" he said.

"Well, we're having a barbecue at my house and I wondered if you could come. . . ."

"A barbecue? Well, I don't know."

"It's okay if you can't," I said quickly.

"No, I can come," he said. "I'd like to come."

"You would?"

"Sure. How do I get to your house?"

"Well, I better draw you a map, and I'll give it to you tomorrow—how's that?" I said.

"That's fine."

"Well," I said, "I guess I'll see you tomorrow. Sorry if I interrupted y'all." I started backing away from him.

"That's all right."

I backed right into a bulletin board on the wall and knocked some papers off. "Oh, no!" I cried. I was so nerve-wracked I nearly broke down as I stooped to retrieve them.

"Don't worry," Joe said. He knelt down and helped me pick up the fallen papers. "There," he said as we stood up.

"Well, thanks a lot for the invitation."

"Sure," I said. "I—I guess I'll see you later."

"Okay," he said, then he touched my hair lightly " 'Bye, honey."

Honey. At least he'd said honey. " 'Bye," I said, and I turned and hurried through the shadows till I found the stage door.

I felt hysterical as I drove home—what in the world had I gone and done? I half cried and half laughed as I shouted, "You idiot! You idiot!" Meaning myself. I couldn't believe it. A barbecue! We'd never had a barbecue my whole life! We weren't that type of family. The most we ever did on the Fourth of July was watch a ball game and maybe go to the high school after dark to see the fireworks. We hadn't even used our patio grill in about three years!

When I got home I was in a state of shock. I walked

right back to my room and lay down on my bed. "Mama!"
I called after a minute.

My mother came to my door. I must have looked sick.
"What's wrong? Are you sick?" she said.

"I'm in shock," I said, tears welling up in my eyes.

"What?"

"I'm in shock," I repeated.

"Why?"

"I just asked Joe Brady to come to our house on the
Fourth of July. I told him we were having a barbecue—"

"A barbecue?" Mama said.

"Yes! A *barbecue!*"

"We're not having a barbecue," she said.

"Well, we have to have one now because I invited him!
Please, Mama!" The tears started spilling out of my eyes.

"That's the day after tomorrow," she said.

"I know it is! Help me—"

"Okay, okay, don't cry, Sunny. You've cried more in
the last two days than I've seen you cry in a whole year."

"I know. My life was never so complicated before!"

"I'll agree with that."

"What can we do?"

"Well, I guess we can cook hamburgers out on the
grill."

"With some barbecue sauce?"

"I don't see why not."

"Oh, God . . ." I lay back on my bed and stared at my
ceiling; I wanted my mother to take charge of everything.

"You get some rest; we'll plan things tomorrow," she said.

"But you have work tomorrow," I said, starting up.

"No, we just have half a day. When I come home we'll get organized."

"Thank you," I said weakly.

"Now get some rest. I think you need it," she said.

"I do. I need it." I closed my eyes with despair. About the only thought that brought me peace was thinking that Joe had seemed to like hearing about my family and my life in Wheeler; maybe his visit would actually bring us close again.

The next day my mother and I prepared the house for Joe's visit. The first thing I wanted to get rid of was the dog's bed in the family room—it was covered with white and black hairs and had a disgusting chewed-up rubber hamburger in it. I carried it back to the laundry room with the dog following after me. "Sleep in here from now on!" I commanded him.

Next I attacked all the newspapers and magazines stacked near the fireplace and all the family pictures everywhere. There were more silly pictures of me—baby pictures and school pictures. Mama helped me carry about half of them back to the hall closet; then we gathered up all the newspapers and magazines and hauled them off to the basement. After that Mama vacuumed while I swept off the furniture on the patio.

"What are you doing?" Larry called from the kitchen window.

"Cleaning."

"You getting paid for it?"

"No, dummy, it's for company tomorrow. We're gonna eat out here on the patio."

"What company?"

"Joe Brady."

"Who is he, anyway?"

"A TV star, that's who."

"You're lying."

"Wait and see."

"It's supposed to rain."

"Shut up—it won't." I stopped sweeping and looked up at the sky. My blood went cold at the thought of rain. I could just picture all of us squeezed around the kitchen table under the overhead lamp, listening to the faucet drip and telling the dog to get down. It was a terrible vision.

I went back into the house and yelled at Mama above the roar of the vacuum cleaner, "What if it rains?"

She cut off the machine. "What?"

"What if it rains?"

"I guess we'll have to eat in the kitchen then."

"Oh, but it's so awful in there!"

The two of us went back to the kitchen to see if it was as awful as I'd thought it was. When we passed through the family room, Larry was sitting on the sofa hunched over his glasses as he cleaned them. I groaned inwardly at the thought of presenting him to Joe. "Sit up straight," I told him.

"Drop dead," he said, and he put his glasses on. "Hey, what happened to all the pictures in here?"

"Don't worry about it," I said.

Mama and I sat at the kitchen table. She suggested which chair might give Joe the best view, and she said she'd get Dad to fix the drippy faucet. "If we take the window fan out of the window, more light'll come in," she said.

"Oh, I don't know. . . ." I said in a worried voice.

"I think it'll help," she said. "Oh! What would you think if I made a strawberry cake?"

"That'd be good." I had to smile at her. As selfish as I was, I wasn't blind to the fact that she could be pretty great sometimes.

19

After work that night I got the map I'd made for Joe, and I waited near the backstage door for him. I was wishing Donna and Jennifer would hurry up and leave, but they seemed to be taking forever. The two of them were still bopping around when I finally caught sight of Joe. Before he saw me, I walked quickly out to the lobby so I could try and catch him alone.

I waited a while, but he didn't appear. I went back to the entrance of the theater and peered in. He was talking with John Wells, Jennifer, and Donna.

I headed right for them. When Joe saw me coming, I thought he looked a little guilty. "Hi," he said.

"Hi," I said without smiling.

"Oh, Donna!" Jennifer squealed, and she playfully slapped Donna's hand. I knew she was just trying to detract attention from me. It didn't work, though. Joe moved away from them and stepped over to me.

"I have your map," I said.

"Oh, you do? Good."

"Here."

He took the map from me and walked over to a wall light to get a better look at it. I followed him and stood close to him—real close, so Donna and Jennifer could get the picture about us.

"Joe!" Donna called. I whipped around, furious at her for interrupting us. Joe held up his hand as if telling her to wait.

"Joe!" she yelled again. He sighed and looked over at her.

"Tell Jennifer that joke you told me," Donna said.

"What joke?"

"About the apes."

"Oh, later," he said.

I froze. What did he mean "later"? He looked back at the map. "I think I can figure it out from this," he said after a moment. "What time should I come?"

"Well, how about noon?"

"That sounds fine."

I stared at him; I couldn't just say good-bye now and walk off, leaving him with those two vultures.

He must have read my mind. "I'll walk you to your car," he said.

"Oh, thanks," I said faintly.

As I walked stiffly down the hall and through the lobby with him, I didn't say much. When we got out to my car, he said, "Thanks for making me the map, Sunny."

I was dying to kiss him or touch him, anything, but I guess I was too inhibited by my worries about us. "You're welcome," I said.

He opened my car door and I slipped down into the driver's seat.

"Good night," he said.

" 'Night," I said. Then I closed the door.

When I was halfway across the parking lot, I stopped the car and looked anxiously back over my shoulder. I couldn't tell if he'd gone back into the theater or not.

I fought back tears on my ride home. I wanted so much for Joe to behave like he used to—looking for me, touching me, saying sexy things. Now it was as if he'd lost interest in me completely, at least as far as sex was concerned.

My last chance to get him back would be tomorrow, I thought. I pictured the two of us taking a walk in the woods back of my house. If we could just spend some time alone, maybe we could break through this wall that had grown up between us. I felt like I mainly just needed to prove to him that I wasn't as inexperienced and naive as I might have led him to believe the other night.

When I got home, I was too anxious to go to bed. "I think I'll step out for a little while," I said to my parents.

"What for?" Dad said. I was surprised—he'd never been in the habit of questioning my comings and goings.

"To visit Ray."

"It's late," he said.

"*Daddy,*" I said.

"Go on." He looked back at the TV. I shook my head at my mother as if to say Daddy was acting nutty, and I headed on outside.

As I climbed the hill, the air felt real warm and humid; I couldn't see any stars in the sky. Please don't let that mean rain, I begged. When I got to Ray's, I was disappointed to see his car was gone. I didn't want to go home and be alone with my nerves, so I sat on his porch and waited for a while.

I could see the TV was on next door at Debbie and Boyd's. I hardly ever visited with the two of them anymore. It was sort of a shame—in high school the three of us used to have a good time together. We'd ride around in Boyd's car after school, eat onion rings at the A & W, and sneak beers every now and then. They were only two years older than me, but now that they were married, it seemed more like twenty.

On a sudden impulse I stood up and headed across the dirt to their house. I didn't know if it was just my restlessness getting to me or if it was my memories of the old days, but I wanted to visit with the two of them. I went up the front steps and rang their bell.

"Lord, what are you doing here?" Debbie said a moment later when she answered the door.

"I just thought I'd drop by."

"Well, what a shock. Come on in, we're watching the news." She led me through the hall and back through the kitchen. All their appliances were covered with lime-green crocheted covers. My mother had taught Debbie how to crochet last winter. "Look who's here," she said to Boyd when we got to the TV room at the back of the house.

"Who? Oh, Sunny. Hi, Sunny," Boyd said.

"Hey, Boyd."

"Have a seat," Debbie said. "Can I get you a Tab?"

"Sure, that'd be good."

Debbie left the room. Boyd looked over at me and said, "How's your job at the dinner theater?"

"Good."

"You eat all that food every night?"

"No, we have a small dinner in the kitchen."

"That roast beef there was good," he said.

"It is good. How's the Winn Dixie?"

"Good."

"Here," Debbie said, coming back into the room. She put our Tabs down and held out a jar of peanuts. "Have some."

"No, thank you."

"Oh, that's how you stay so skinny." She settled down next to me on the sofa. I'd expected her to start chatting, but she just stared at the TV. I hadn't meant to brag about Joe Brady, but I'm afraid my need to make myself feel more secure about him got the best of me. I pretended to yawn, then I said, "Hey, guess what."

Neither of them seemed to hear me.

I pinched Debbie's arm. "Guess what."

"Ouch—what?"

"Guess who's coming to our house for lunch tomorrow."

"Who?"

"Joe Brady."

Her eyes got huge. Other than that her face didn't change expression. "What for?"

"We've gotten to be close lately—if you know what I mean."

"How close?"

"Well, we've been dating."

"You have?"

"Yeah."

Debbie stared at me for a moment, then she turned to Boyd. "Did you hear that?" she said.

Boyd was engrossed in the news. "Boyd," Debbie said, her voice sounding strained. I think she was jealous. "Boyd!" He looked over at her. "Sunny's going to have that TV star over for lunch tomorrow. They've been dating."

Boyd nodded, then he went back to the television.

"Well, Ida Faye'll have a conniption," Debbie said. As

she ate the rest of her peanuts, her shoulders were sort of hunched up around her ears. I thought she'd gained even more weight recently.

"Where's Ray?" I said after a minute.

"Who knows?" Debbie said.

As the three of us just sat there watching the news, I began to feel pretty lonely. Finally I got up off the sofa and said, "Well, I better be going."

"Okay. 'Bye," Debbie said.

"I'll see y'all," I said to her, then I turned to Boyd. His eyes were closed and his mouth had dropped open.

"Forget him—he's dead to the world," Debbie said.

"Well, tell him 'bye for me," I said, and I headed quickly for the front door and escaped into the warm night air.

I was almost down to the street when I heard a car door slam. "Is that you?" I said.

I heard Ray laugh. "Is that you?" he said.

"Yes!" I felt so happy, I nearly tripped over the hedge to get to him—now here was somebody I could really depend on! I found him opening up the back of his station wagon. "I was looking for you earlier!" I said.

"You were?"

"Yes. I'm glad you came back."

He chuckled. "Did you think I'd run off somewhere?"

"Oh, no—I'd kill you if you had."

He heaved a guitar case out of the back of his car. "Look what I've got," he said.

"What is it?"

"My new guitar."

"You're kidding! What kind did you get?"

"A Martin D-18."

"Is it a good one?"

"Yeah, it's real good."

"Oh, I want to hear it!"

"Come on up to the porch."

I followed Ray up to his porch, and we sat down on the steps in the dark. He opened the case and pulled out the guitar, then set it across his knees. He spent a couple of minutes tuning it up, then played a short song.

"It sounds good!" I said.

"Yeah, it's sweet."

"Well, now what are you going to do with it—that's what I want to know."

"What do you mean?"

"I mean are you planning to go out there and play music again, or what?"

"I don't know."

"You think you'd like to play solo or with a band?"

"I don't know that either."

"Let me ask you something," I said. I knew I was about to take a risk asking about his past. Ray never talked to anyone about his past and about all the problems he'd had, but I was in the mood to talk seriously with him. "Are you afraid to be a musician again?"

I heard him suck in his breath. "Come on now, talk to me," I said. "Don't you wish you were out there playing again?"

"Yeah, I guess so."

"Then why in the world don't you?"

"I guess I don't trust myself."

"Trust yourself about what, Ray?"

He shrugged.

"Come on, trust yourself about what, dummy?"

"Well, when you're on the road and playing at all these places, you get tempted. . . ." He stopped.

"Tempted with drugs and all?"

"More or less."

"But can't you just say no, if you don't want to do them anymore?" I said.

"I don't know. It's easy to lose control in certain kinds of environments."

"What kind of environments?"

"Oh, being on the road, partying a lot, playing on stage. . . . I lose control."

"You think that happens to everybody?"

"I guess some people do all right."

"I bet you could be one of them," I said. "Not that I don't understand what you mean. I know what it's like to lose control."

He smiled. "What makes you lose control?" he said.

"My feelings."

"Oh, yeah. You've always had a temper, Sunny."

"Yeah, I know that, but I can also lose my head over liking people too."

"Yeah?"

"Oh, yeah, sure."

"That happens when you're young—"

"Oh, Ray! Don't you go making out that I'm so young —I've had about enough of that now!"

"But you are." He laughed.

I raised my hand to hit him. He caught it and held on to it. "It makes me so mad when you act like I'm so young!" I said.

"I don't—"

"You do!" He was still holding my hand. I didn't know if it was because he meant to or if it was because he'd just gotten stuck with it. I got it back from him by giving him a little shove. "I wish you'd change your view of me," I said.

"I've got a good view of you."

"Oh, sure you do." I gave him another little shove. "Hey, play 'Mamas, Don't Let Your Babies Grow Up to Be Cowboys.' "

"Okay."

As he played the song, my stomach started churning again, thinking about tomorrow—I'd actually forgotten about it while I'd been talking with Ray. I hoped Joe wouldn't expect me to play this song on the guitar. I felt jittery as I stood up. "Well, I better get home," I said. "There's a few things I want to do before tomorrow. We're having company for the Fourth."

"Oh, yeah?"

I debated a second whether or not to tell him all about Joe Brady and all my fears, but I decided not to. Ray had actually seemed to be a little jealous the other day when

Ida Faye and I had gone on about Joe. "Well, 'bye," I said.

"Who's coming?" he said as I started off.

"Just that soap opera actor from the dinner theater. Well, see you later. I love your new guitar!"

"Thanks."

"Good night."

"G'night."

I was in better spirits as I headed home. I loved the fact that Ray had talked to me about his past. All of a sudden I heard him really cut loose on his guitar. I stopped on the dark road and listened. He'd wake the whole neighborhood if he kept that up, I thought. But then suddenly it was quiet again and all you could hear was crickets.

20

At eleven-forty-five the next morning it was raining. I sat in the living room, staring in despair out the picture window. I was wearing a green skirt and a print blouse. I'd spent a long time trying to find an outfit that looked simple and natural. I'd also tried to pick out the right garments for my family to wear; I'd gone from one closet to the next, making suggestions. My parents hadn't seemed to mind, but Larry had gotten mad at me—he'd said I was off my rocker and he'd taken off for a friend's house. It was just as well, I thought. He would have asked Joe a lot of questions about his soap opera—even though I'd instructed the whole family not to do that. My father had also been instructed not to bring up the subject of me spending the night with Joe. I hadn't really been that afraid that he would—it was hard to imagine my dad being rude to a guest.

I could hear the pressure cooker gauge knocking in the kitchen. Mama was making spaghetti sauce since we couldn't cook on the patio. I heard the TV go on in the family room. I stood up to holler at Daddy to turn it off, but then I sat back down. I was too nervous to worry about the TV now.

When I saw Joe's Volkswagen coming down our block, my heart nearly stopped. I watched him slow down in front of the house, back up, then turn into the driveway. When his car door slammed, the dog started barking. I rushed into the family room and told my dad to get the dog. I'd put him in the laundry room a half hour ago, but someone must have let him out. The doorbell rang, and the dog dashed to the front of the house yipping. I charged into the kitchen and squealed at Mama to get the dog. She dropped the head of lettuce she was holding and took off after him—she must have sensed I was about to fly apart.

After Mama carried the dog away, I opened the door. "Hi, Joe," I said.

"Hi," he said.

"Happy Fourth of July." I laughed nervously. "Come on in."

I held the door for him as he stepped in. He looked wonderful in a pair of gray pants and a black shirt. "Let's go in here," I said.

I led him through the sitting room into the family room. My dad stood up when we came in. "This is my father, Vernon Dickens," I said. "Daddy, this is Joe Brady."

"Hi, Mr. Dickens," Joe said, shaking Dad's hand.

"Pleased to meet you," Dad said.

"Did you have a hard time finding our address?" I asked Joe.

"No. No problem." He shook his head at me and then he shook his head at my dad.

When Daddy didn't make any response, I said, "Well! I'm gonna turn this down." I walked over to the TV and turned it down. I didn't turn it all the way off because now I thought it was needed to help fill up the silence. "I wonder what's taking Mama so long," I said.

"She's coming," Dad said.

"Hi," my mother said a few seconds later, coming into the room.

"Hi there!" I sounded like I was greeting her for the first time in a week. "This is Joe Brady. Joe, this is my mother, Rose Dickens."

Joe and my mother said hello to each other. "Would you like to have a seat?" she asked him.

"Sure. Thanks," he said.

Joe and I sat down on the sofa. My dad leaned back in his recliner and his eyes sort of wandered to the television. A baseball game was on. "Vernon," Mama said, "can you get Joe something to drink?"

"Would you like a Coke?" my dad said.

"Sure, that would be fine," Joe said.

My parents went into the kitchen. Joe looked at me and smiled; I thought he was feeling a little awkward. I certainly was. It was so weird to be sitting with him in my own living room. It was like a dream and reality coming together. I felt very hot. "We were going to have a barbecue outside," I said.

He nodded.

"But now we're having spaghetti."

"Sounds good."

"It is good. My mother makes good spaghetti sauce."

Dad came back with a Coke for Joe. He handed it to him, and he asked me if I'd wanted a Coke too. I told him no thanks.

Dad sat back in his chair, then looked at Joe. "What's your weather like up in New York this time of year?" he said.

"It's pretty nice," Joe said.

"Is it real hot?" Dad said.

"Not really. Not now, anyway. It gets pretty hot in late July and August."

Dad nodded, then looked back at the baseball game. A moment later he turned to Joe. "How hot does it get?" he said.

I almost giggled. I couldn't help it. I knew he was doing his best, but it was pitiful.

"It can get up in the nineties," Joe said.

Dad nodded, then looked back at the TV.

"Who's playing?" Joe said.

Dad didn't seem to hear him.

"Who's playing, Daddy?" I said loudly.

Dad smiled at Joe over his shoulder. "The Mets and the Braves," he said.

"Oh, really?" Joe sat forward a little and stared at the TV. I looked at it too. The only problem was the sound was turned down so low you could barely hear it. But I guessed my father thought that it would be rude for him to turn it up louder. It might have been rude, but it would have been a lot better than the three of us straining to hear.

"Lunch is ready," my mother said finally.

My father sort of grunted and heaved himself up out of his chair. We all filed into the kitchen. The table was all laid out under the bright overhead lamp. Mama told us to sit and she poured our iced teas. When she sat down, my parents bowed their heads.

Joe didn't seem to know what was going on till my mother said, "Thank you, Lord, for this food . . ." but then he bowed his head too.

"And for all thy blessings. Amen," she said.

"Amen," my father said.

"Go ahead and serve yourselves," Mama said.

We started passing the bowls and serving ourselves. My hand was a little shaky as I buttered my French bread. I didn't know how I was going to eat considering the state my nerves were in. I still felt very hot. Joe looked so handsome sitting at our table that I almost couldn't look at him. My parents must have felt the same way, because they seemed to be concentrating unusually hard on their food.

Suddenly the dog barked this funny bark from the laundry room. My dad and I laughed. "He knows we're eating," Dad said.

Mama nodded and smiled.

The dog yapped again and we all giggled again, even Joe. It seems odd, but from then on it was a more easy-going meal. Every time the dog barked it gave us a chance to laugh and let off some of the nervousness we were experiencing.

We were just starting to eat our strawberry cake when the doorbell rang. Mama went to answer it. I heard her talking; then I heard Debbie's voice. A moment later the two of them came into the kitchen.

"Hi, y'all!" Debbie exclaimed. Her eyes rested on Joe Brady. "Hi, Mr. Brady," she said.

"Hi," Joe said.

"I bet he don't remember me," she said to us. "I got your autograph backstage at the dinner theater, and I got one for Sunny too! Didn't I, Sunny?"

I just stared at her.

"Sunny was chicken!" Debbie said, grinning a big toothy smile at Joe. I swear I could have shot her.

21

"Would you like a piece of cake?" my mother asked Debbie.

"Oh, I don't want to barge in on y'all," Debbie said.

"You're not," Mama said.

"Well, then I'd love some cake." She sat down and Mama served her a piece. "Oh, it's real good," Debbie said after she took a big bite. She looked at Joe—her eyes were as big as doorknobs. "I used to watch you on *Another Love*," she said.

Oh, no, I thought, he hates this kind of thing.

"Really?" he said.

"Yes!" Debbie said. "Now why don't you get back on it?"

"Because my character was killed," Joe said.

She laughed loudly. "Well, you can come back as your twin brother, can't you? That happened with Marco on *One Life to Live!*"

"Debbie—" I said.

But she was all wound up now. "Ida Faye—that's my husband's grandmother—she watched you all the time too! She adores you! Did Sunny ever tell you that?"

"Debbie, cool it," I said.

"I was up at Ida Faye's just now," she said, "and when I told her you were here, she nearly had a conniption! She'd love it if you was to pop in on her—if Sunny was to let you, that is."

This was the limit. "No, Debbie, we don't have time," I said.

"You don't?"

"No!"

"You don't have time?" Debbie asked Joe.

"Well . . ." He seemed uncomfortable. He probably didn't want to get caught in the middle of some fuss between me and Debbie, and I didn't blame him.

"Do you?" she asked him again.

"Quit, Debbie. Quit asking him," I said.

"Well, is there any law against asking?" she said.

"No, there's no law." I looked to my mother for help, but she just looked embarrassed.

"Well, I just think it would be something if Joe could stop in and say hi to her," Debbie said. "You know it would be the highlight of her life."

I sighed. She was going to worry us to death unless I consented. "You want to go up there? It's just a few doors away," I asked Joe.

"Sure," he said.

I stood up and shoved my chair into place.

Debbie asked my mother to please save the rest of her piece of cake for later; then the three of us left the house.

The rain had stopped, but it was still gray and drippy as we started up the street. "Did Tina know you were with the mob?" Debbie asked Joe. "I mean in real life did anyone ever tell her?"

"Debbie," I said. "He doesn't like to talk about the soap opera all the time."

"That's okay," Joe said. "Who do you mean—the actress who played Tina, or the character Tina?"

"Um—the actress," Debbie said.

"Well, sure the actress knew," Joe said. "But I wasn't really with the mob, you know. That was just the story in the soap."

"Oh, that's right," Debbie said, as if she'd forgotten that the story was make-believe.

When we got to Ida Faye's, Ray was just getting out of his car. "Hey Ray, meet Joe Brady!" Debbie said, leading Joe over to meet Ray. She was really acting like she was in charge, I thought furiously.

Before they got to Ray, the front door opened and Ida

Faye stepped out onto the porch. "Lookey here!" Debbie
shouted at her. "I brought you a present!"

Ida Faye laughed like she was embarrassed but pleased.
Debbie steered Joe over to the porch to introduce him to
Ida Faye. I was so angry I turned my back on all of them
and glared out at the street.

"Hey—" Ray said, walking up to me.

I didn't look at him.

"Hey, you."

"What?"

"What's eating you?"

"I'm just mad, that's all."

"Why?"

"I'm furious with your sister-in-law for dragging my
date up here, that's why!"

Ray looked at the porch. "It seems like Grandma's
happy to see him," he said.

"Well, who wouldn't be? He's a *TV star*!" I snapped.

"Hey—whoa," Ray said, backing up a step.

But I just ignored him as I whirled around and watched
Debbie and Joe leave the porch. Ida Faye was waving
good-bye to Joe as I headed over to them. "Thank you,
Joe," Debbie said.

"Sure."

"We have to go now," I said sharply to Debbie, and I
touched Joe's elbow. I didn't say a word more as I led him
across the yard. I caught Ray watching me, but I looked
away. I was sure he was disappointed in me for acting
so ugly, but I couldn't help myself at the moment.

As we headed down the hill to my house, I apologized to Joe for Debbie's dragging him to Ida Faye's. "That's okay," he said. "She seems like a nice lady."

"She is." I assumed he meant Ida Faye and not Debbie. It wasn't that I minded Joe visiting Ida Faye; in fact, I wanted him to visit with her. I probably would have taken him there myself. I was really just mad at Debbie for barging in and carrying on as if Joe was some precious gem or something!

The sun was starting to come out, making the air real steamy. The woods would be all hot and wet—we might be real uncomfortable walking back there, I thought—but this was my last chance. "Would you like to take a little walk?" I asked Joe.

He glanced at his watch. "Sure, I have some time," he said.

After we'd walked about half a block, I suggested we turn into the woods. "There's a path that's real nice," I said. "I practically lived back there when I was a kid."

"Oh yeah? What did you do back here?" Joe said as he followed me into the woods.

"My brother and I had a little fort," I said. "It's gone now, but I still come here sometimes." This wasn't the truth—I hadn't been back here in ages, but I didn't want him to think I was up to something sneaky.

The leaves were dripping and the ground was real wet —we wouldn't be able to lie down, I thought frantically. That might be okay if we could just sit on a log or something, as long as we could get physically close. I didn't see a good log, but we did come to a wide tree stump that had enough room for two.

"Oh, this is a good place to rest," I said, sitting on the damp stump.

Joe stood near me and looked up at the trees. I stared at his handsome face, and then I reached out and put my hand on his wrist. "Sit down here," I said.

He looked at me. "There's no room," he said.

I should have stopped there, but I didn't. "Sure, there is," I said, trying to sound flirtatious.

"No, Sunny—"

"Okay, then—" I got up and stood close to him. I put my hands on his arms and suddenly I leaned over and kissed him. It was the type of thing he'd done to me just a few days ago, but he only half-heartedly kissed me back, and he didn't put his arms around me or anything.

"You're not in the mood?" I said when he pulled away.

"I guess not," he said.

"Oh. Well, I am. . . ." I laughed. A wave of horror began to wash over me.

"Don't, Sunny."

"Don't what?" I felt like I was drowning.

"Act this way—it's not very sexy," he said.

"It's not?"

He took my hand. "Come on, let's go back," he said, and he started to lead me out of the woods. Thick waves of pain rolled over me as the birds sang like crazy in the rain-soaked bushes.

22

I felt numb as Joe thanked me and my parents and we all said good-bye. I felt numb after he drove off in his car, and I went back into the house and sat on the sofa next to my mother and just stared at the ball game.

I started to lose my numbness, though, when I sensed Mama was watching me. "He's nice," she said.

I just nodded.

"Did you enjoy yourself?" she said.

"Oh, yes," I said. Then I added carefully, "Excuse me," and I got up and went out to the front porch. I was so humiliated I felt like I was on fire. Suddenly I jumped off the porch and headed blindly up the hill to Debbie's.

When I got to her house I rang her bell, but there was no answer even though her car was in the driveway. I banged on the door and shouted, "Debbie!"

"She took Grandma to the store," Ray said. I hadn't even noticed him working in his yard.

"Well, what's her car doing here?" I yelled.

"She drove Grandma's."

"Damn!" I kicked Debbie's door.

"Take it easy," Ray said.

"Oh, mind your own business, Ray!"

"Hey, what's wrong with you?" He started toward me.

"I'm mad at Debbie!"

"What for? For stealing your date?"

"She didn't steal him—you think he'd be interested in her? Ha! It's because she wrecked our lunch! She treated him like he was some god or something!"

"She didn't know any better," Ray said.

"Well, that's no excuse! She's going to pay for it, too!" I kicked her door again.

Ray jumped up onto the porch. "Hey—don't act so crazy!"

"Oh, go to hell, Ray!"

He grabbed my arms. "Stop talking like that! What's the matter with you?"

"I love him! That's what!" Tears flooded my eyes.

Ray didn't say anything for a few seconds. He just let go of me. "Oh. Well, I didn't know that," he said. He put his hands in his pockets and walked a few steps away. He leaned against a porch column and laughed.

"Why are you laughing?"

"I don't know, it just seems sort of like a funny kind of love to me," he said.

"What's so funny about it?"

Ray shrugged. "You hardly know him."

"I know him better than you think! I spent the night with him!"

Ray looked out at the street. "That doesn't mean anything," he said in a quiet voice.

"Why do you say that?"

"It just doesn't. You don't mean anything to him, Sunny."

"What are you saying that for, Ray?" Tears started down my face. "Don't you think he likes me? What's wrong with me?"

"I didn't say he doesn't like you. I'm just saying that he's passing through town. When you're in show business you meet lots of girls, and when they fall for you, you sleep with them—or whatever—but it doesn't mean anything. You're just using them."

"Joe didn't use me, Ray!"

"Seems like he did. And it seems like you're just raising hell because your pride got hurt—"

"Oh, you don't know everything!" I yelled.

"I know show business."

"No you don't, Ray—not this kind! The kind you knew was all full of drugs and things like that!"

"Oh, yeah?"

"Yeah! You told me so yourself last night! Joe's world is different from what you knew! You couldn't even take that life you were living—so you just quit and came running home!"

"Watch it—" Ray said.

"You watch it! This isn't like the show business you were in. It's not down in the gutter like that! Joe's not like you, Ray!"

Ray just stared at me. Then he sort of laughed by blowing air out of his nostrils, and he stepped down from the porch and started off.

"Where you going?" I said.

He didn't answer or look back as he walked away under the trees.

"Are you mad?" I said.

"Yeah."

"Well, I'm mad too! And you got it wrong about something else," I said. "Joe Brady didn't even try to make love when I slept with him. I just lay beside him all night and we didn't do a thing! See—he's not out to use me, Ray!"

"Right," Ray said. I couldn't tell if he was being sarcastic or not. A moment later his screen door slammed.

I was in agony the rest of the afternoon. I felt horrible about my fight with Ray. And I hated myself for acting like such an idiot in the woods! "It's not very sexy when you act this way"—those words made me want to tear my hair out. And telling him I was in the mood! I lay on my bed and wept, I was so mortified.

Finally I dragged myself up and started getting ready for work. My face looked hideous staring back at me in the mirror; my eyes were red and puffy. I figured I'd hurry away after the show tonight as quickly as I could so Joe wouldn't see me.

I avoided looking at my parents as I passed quickly through the family room. "I'll be right home after work," I said.

"You don't have a date?" my mother called. I knew she was just saying this to make some contact with me, but her words were like arrows in my back.

"I don't think so," I hollered back, and I headed out the door.

I stepped into the yard just in time to see Ray's station wagon coming down the street. He didn't even glance in my direction when he passed our house. From the way he was holding his head, I could tell he was making a point of it not to look. "I hate you too," I muttered. But then I shuddered—I didn't think I could bear it if Ray Perkins had turned against me too.

My eyes stung as I got in my car and backed out of the driveway. I dreaded going in to work. On the ride out to the mall, I examined my face in the car mirror. I was horrified to see how swollen my eyes were.

When I got to the theater, I tried not to look at anyone as I hurried into the kitchen and grabbed a couple of ice cubes. I put them in a cloth napkin and rushed to the ladies' room. Just as I opened the door I caught sight of Donna and Jennifer sitting on the counter. It was too late to turn around without making a fool of myself, so I just walked past them and went into a stall. I locked the door and just stood there, pressing the ice cubes against my eyelids.

Donna and Jennifer kept right on talking about one of their favorite topics—their sex lives—and being in the position I was in, I was forced to listen.

"We weren't in there five minutes before he came at me," Jennifer said.

Donna squealed. "Oh, how was it?" she said.

"What do you think? We made love all night. We didn't sleep a wink."

Donna clapped. I hated them both—they were carrying on especially for my benefit, I felt.

"Was he good?" Donna said.

"Was he good?"

I mimicked her silently—she made me want to gag.

"What'd y'all do this morning?" Donna said.

"We went to breakfast."

"Where?"

"Here at the mall—the Fancy Coffee Shop."

My heart stopped. I took the ice off my eyes.

"What'd you do after that?" Donna said.

"He took me home. He had to go to some barbecue," Jennifer said.

Everything started to go black—

"Where?" Donna said.

"Wheeler."

Suddenly I burst out of my stall like an animal. The first thing I did was hurl my pieces of ice at Jennifer's head. Then I leaped across the room like a kangaroo and attacked her. She screamed, and Donna screamed too and started hitting me on the back. I yanked Jennifer off her perch on the counter and Donna pushed me, knocking me and Jennifer over, and the two of us fell down on the floor. We were on the floor pounding each other and swearing when the door opened, and the next thing I knew Mr. Swank was grabbing hold of my arms and pulling me off her. I can still hear Suzanne saying in a high voice, "Oh, my! Oh, my! This is insane!"

Somehow I got pulled to my feet and steered out of the bathroom down the corridor to the office. Mr. Swank was on one side of me and Linda on the other. Suzanne must have stayed behind to talk to Jennifer and Donna. I was led into the office and told by Mr. Swank to sit down and cool off.

A couple of minutes later Suzanne came into the office and talked with Mr. Swank in the other room; then they both came to me. Mr. Swank asked if I'd started the fight and I said yes. When he asked me why, I just mumbled that the two of them had made me mad.

Mr. Swank said he was sorry but he'd have to let me go. I nodded, and then someone handed me my pocketbook. I stood up and crossed to the door.

Suzanne led me out to the promenade. "Sunny, I'm really sorry this had to happen," she said.

"Me, too," I said.

She closed the heavy wooden door behind me and it clicked into place—locking me out of paradise forever.

23

I hardly remember the next few hours after I left the theater. I know that I wandered up and down the promenade of the mall, and at one point I took a dollar bill from my pocketbook and bought a Breyer's ice cream cone, and when I was through with that one, I bought another one. I remember that I sat on a white plastic bench next to a woman who complained about her feet, and I told her about the Dr. Scholl shoes my mother wears and I suggested she try to find some at Kinney's. I remember I talked my head off until the woman's husband joined her —and then I left them and started down the promenade back toward the theater.

I arrived at the theater just after the show had ended. I slipped into Waterbed City and watched the crowd come out. When the last of the audience had left, Suzanne undid the door stopper and pulled the door shut. It was just a matter of time now before Joe would appear. I tried to prepare myself for seeing him with Jennifer. I had enough sense to know better than to attack her again, but the truth was I wasn't that concerned about her anymore. I just wanted to see Joe Brady—I had no idea what shape the fire in me would take when I laid eyes on him.

The door opened and John and Joe came out. It was only the two of them. I watched them talk for a few seconds. Then Joe took off by himself. I followed him out to the parking lot, and after he'd driven off, I ran to my car.

When I pulled into Joe's apartment complex, I saw his car sitting empty in its usual spot. I parked and went into the building. I took the elevator up to his floor and walked down the carpeted hallway and knocked on his door.

A few seconds later Joe opened the door. "Oh," he said. "Hi, Sunny." From the look on his face, I could tell he wasn't all that happy to see me.

"Hi."

We both just stood there for a moment. Then he said, "Do you want to come in?"

I nodded, and he stepped aside to let me in. I walked right into his living room.

"Are you going to beat me up too?" he said with a little smile.

I didn't answer.

He closed the door, then walked over to the couch and sat down.

When he looked at me, I said, "Have you been sleeping with Jennifer all along?"

"No. Last night was the first time."

"Oh. Well, at least I know that what a friend of mine said about you is true."

Joe leaned back as if he was trying to appear relaxed. "What did your friend say about me, Sunny?" he said.

"He said that you were just passing through town, spending time with different girls, but that none of them really mattered to you. You were just using them."

"That's not true." He leaned forward and rested his elbows on his knees and stared at me intensely. "You meant something to me."

"Oh, well, does Jennifer mean something to you too?"

"No, not really."

"So you just make love to the girls who don't matter to you—and not to the ones who do?"

Joe sighed and ran his fingers back through his hair. "Look, Sunny, I thought you were different—"

"But you lost interest in me when you discovered I was a virgin."

"What?"

"You lost interest in me when you thought you shouldn't sleep with me."

"Is that what you think?"

"Well, what should I think?"

"I didn't mind that about you. In fact, I was sort of surprised when you were so quick to change."

I dreaded what he was about to say next. "What do you mean—like in the woods today?"

"Well, you came on pretty strong the other morning too."

I felt sick. "You mean *that's* what you didn't like?"

"I just didn't think that you were that way."

"What way?" I yelled suddenly. He looked startled. "What way? You mean you got turned off because I acted passionate? You stopped liking me when you discovered I liked you enough to want to make love with you? Oh, that's awful! That's so mean!" He looked astonished. But I was the one who was the most astonished. "You have no idea what I'm really like! I'm not at all the sweet innocent little lamb you tried to make me out as! You don't know me at all!"

"I guess I don't," he said.

"Boy, it's like we were just acting parts in a play, wasn't it? You thought I was somebody that I wasn't. But don't feel bad. I didn't know who you were either. I didn't know you could be so stupid!" I really laughed after saying that. I couldn't stop myself. Tears even came to my eyes.

Joe laughed too, but not much.

Finally I calmed down enough to wipe my eyes and catch my breath. "I'm sorry, I guess I lost it." I sniffed and said, "Well, I better be going now."

"You have to go now?" Something in his voice made me think he wouldn't have minded if I'd wanted to stay longer, but I'm afraid that that prospect didn't interest me much. What did we have to say to each other? Not much. And as for sex with him, the thought just didn't attract me anymore—he seemed so weird about it all. "Yeah, I better go now. I'm due at home—my parents have been worried about me lately."

He stood up as I started across the room. When I grabbed hold of the door knob, I looked back at him. It was odd, but even his good looks didn't do much for me now. "Well, I hope I see you again someday," I said to be nice.

"I'd like that."

"Heck, I'll probably see you in *People* magazine," I said.

He laughed. "God, I hope not," he said.

If he hoped that, I wondered why in the world he was in show business to begin with, but I didn't take the time to ask him. I was in sort of a hurry to get going.

24

I rode down the highway, listening to the radio. I actually felt pretty good. It was like I'd bobbed to the surface of the water I'd been drowning in lately and could breathe again. But the next song on the radio made me feel sad—"Tonight I'll celebrate my love with you. . . ." In a way I wanted to cry—not for the real Joe Brady, but for the one I'd invented. The truth about our romance was actually a little creepy. I don't know how on earth I could have been so wrong.

Farther down the road another song, a real country-type one this time, made me feel bad about Ray Perkins. I'd about wrecked everything with him today. I just prayed he knew me well enough to know I'd been off my rocker lately.

When I got to our street, I drove up the hill to Ray's house. I cursed when I saw that his car wasn't there. I parked anyway and waited for a while. "I'm sorry. Hey, dummy, I'm sorry for acting so ugly," I murmured to the dark, rehearsing what I'd say to him. Finally, though, I was forced to give up and head on home. It was getting late and I didn't want to get my parents started.

When I got into our house, I just said good night to everyone, then went straight back to my room. I figured tomorrow I'd tell them about losing my job and all; I was too beat to do it now.

Tired as I was, though, I couldn't sleep. I couldn't get Ray off my mind. I was so mad at myself. No wonder he didn't confide in people, when friends like me just went and threw it back in his face!

I slept fitfully. As it started to get light, I felt like I couldn't wait a minute longer. I got dressed, then crept out of the house and headed up the street to Ray's.

When I got there I was surprised to see that his car was still gone. I climbed the steps to the porch and knocked lightly. Ida Faye usually got up with the sun. I hoped today was no exception.

It wasn't—when she opened the door a moment later, she was all dressed and even wearing her red apron. "Hey there," she said.

"Hey. I just thought I'd drop by and visit."

"Isn't it a little early to be out visiting?" she said as she held the door open for me.

"What time is it?"

"A quarter to six."

We both laughed. "I guess it is," I said, "but I couldn't sleep."

"Come on back to the kitchen," she said. She sounded as happy as usual to see me. I guessed she hadn't heard about the fight I'd had with Ray. Of course, it wasn't like him to have told her.

As I followed Ida Faye back to the kitchen, her hallway smelled like lilac. This house always smells good, I thought. I didn't know if it was a spray she used or a sachet or what.

"You want some juice?" she said when we got to the kitchen.

"No, thank you." Gospel music was playing on the radio and something was boiling like crazy on the stove. "What's cooking?"

"Jars."

"Jars?"

"I'm putting up some preserves."

"Oh. You boil the little rubber collars too?"

"Yes."

I watched her wipe her hands on her apron. "Where's Ray?" I said offhandedly.

"He took off yesterday."

I held my breath. "Took off?"

"Yes."

"Where did he go?"

"Over to Charlotte."

"What for?"

"He said he was going for a few days to stay with some friends."

"Friends?"

"Yes, I reckon some of his old band people." She poured herself a glass of water. "It worries me," she said as she stared out the window over the sink.

"Why?"

"I don't think much of those fellas. Oh, come look," she said. "Look—there's a hummingbird."

I went over to the window and looked out with her, but all I saw was trees.

"He's sticking his beak in one of the petunias," she said.

"Oh, yeah," I said, though I didn't really see it. I was too upset wondering if Ray had taken off because of our fight. I looked sideways at Ida Faye. Her wrinkled old face was a grayish color today; it looked ancient in the early sunlight. "Why does it worry you?" I said. "A few days isn't so bad."

"What?"

"I'm saying that if Ray's just going to be gone for a few days, why does that worry you?"

"Oh. I guess I'm afraid that it might give him time to fall into some bad habits again."

"Oh, he won't."

"I'm not so sure."

"Why?"

"He seemed so unhappy."

"He did? How could you tell?"

"Oh, I can tell from this look he gets. It's been the same since he was little."

"You think he was feeling bad because of something that happened?"

"I reckon."

"Did it happen yesterday afternoon?" I said.

"I don't know, but probably. He seemed fine earlier."

I felt sick. "Well, one thing's for sure," I said. "He wouldn't want you to worry about him."

"I know. You know, in the year he's been back, he hasn't said one word about what he's been through?"

"He's talked to me a little about it," I said.

"I'm not surprised," she said.

"Why?"

"Oh, because he's so crazy about you."

"He is not! What makes you say that?"

She smiled. "I might be old," she said, "but I'm not deaf and blind."

My heart started pounding in my head. "Well—wh—has he said something to you?" I said.

The front door slammed. "Shhh!" I said.

"Grandma?" Boyd said from the hall. He came into the kitchen. "Hi, Sunny."

"Hi."

"What are you doing up so early?" Ida Faye asked him.

"We're doing an inventory before the store opens."

"Oh."

Boyd and Ida Faye talked about what groceries she wanted him to pick up for her, but my mind was on something else—had *I* been deaf and blind? "Well, I better go," I said, interrupting the two of them. I started backing out of the kitchen. " 'Bye y'all. . . ."

" 'Bye," Ida Faye said. "See you later."

First I went home and woke my mother up. I squatted by her bed and whispered that I was going to drive over to Charlotte today and see Ray, and I'd explain the whole thing to her later.

"Oh, what next, Sunny?" she said, sighing, but then she added, "Be careful on the highway."

It took a couple of hours to drive to Charlotte. I knew how to find the old house where Ray used to live with his music buddies from the times I'd been there a few years back with Debbie and Boyd. It was an old farmhouse about ten miles this side of the city.

The sun was bright as I passed a used car lot I remembered. I turned onto the dirt road just beyond it, then I bumped down the road, passing an old white horse in a field and a house trailer with a clothesline full of clothes.

I didn't know if Ray would be at his old house or not. I didn't even know for sure if his friends still lived there. I remembered when I was out here before, a big brown dog lived on the premises and a couple of other musicians from the band, plus Ray's old girlfriend, Margie, and a blond woman who rode a motorcycle. The blond woman had very pale skin and I believed she was a dancer.

Suddenly the same brown dog from back then bounded out from the bushes beside the road, barking at my car. I rolled up my window and stopped in front of the old wooden house. There were some kids' toys in the yard.

I didn't see Ray's car. Just a beat-up red Impala was parked out front. The dog stood next to my car and kept barking, so I didn't get out. The front door opened and the pale, blond woman I remembered stepped out onto the porch. She was wearing a flimsy nightgown and holding a baby. She called the dog and he went to her.

I rolled down my window and said, "Hi! I'm a friend of Ray Perkins's. Have you seen him by any chance?"

"They went to the store for coffee," she said. She looked worn out. I wondered if she'd given up dancing.

"Well, do you know when he'll be back?" I said.

"Soon."

"You mind if I sit here and wait?"

She shook her head. The baby started crying, so she took it back inside the house. It was depressing.

I listened to the car radio as I waited. Suddenly the dog started barking again. He jumped up from the porch and bounded out of the yard.

I looked over my shoulder. Against the early-morning blue sky, Ray's station wagon was bumping down the road. It stopped about ten feet in back of my car. A bearded guy in a red tank top got out carrying a bag of groceries, but Ray stayed in the car. We stared at one another through our windows.

His bearded friend walked over to me. I recognized him as the drummer in Ray's old band. "Hi," he said. I could tell he didn't remember who I was.

"Hi, I'm a friend of Ray's," I said. "I'm here to see him for a minute."

"Oh, okay." The man looked back at Ray sitting in his car, then he looked at me. He seemed to gather that this was personal. He just nodded, then he went into the house, leaving the big dog out on the porch.

I was probably risking my life with that animal, but I got out of my car and walked over to Ray. The dog held his head up and sniffed the air as he watched me lean against the side of Ray's car. I looked in at Ray and waved two fingers. "Hi there," I said, grinning.

He just looked at me without smiling or saying anything. This was going to be harder than I'd expected.

"Ida Faye told me you were here," I said.

He still didn't say anything.

I turned away and pressed my back against the car. The dog stood up and barked. "Hey, can I sit in your car while we talk?" I said. "I'm afraid of that dog."

Ray nodded.

I went around and got in the passenger side and slammed the door shut behind me. Ray kept looking straight ahead, his hands gripping the bottom of his steering wheel. "How come you're so tense?" I said jokingly.

He shrugged.

"I can't believe *I* make you nervous after all these years," I said.

He looked at me. "What are you doing here?" he said quietly.

"I came to see you."

"What about your TV star?"

"I lost interest in him," I said simply.

He didn't say anything. You could hear the baby crying inside the house, and the dog was barking like crazy on the porch. "What a lot of commotion," I said.

"Yeah, it's a zoo," he said.

"Then what do you want to stay here for?"

He didn't answer as he stared at the house. After a long silence I began to panic. He was being too moody for too long. It occurred to me I might really have made a fool of myself coming all the way out here. "Hey, are you still mad at me?" I said.

He looked over at me. Before he could answer, I went on, "Your grandmother told me you were crazy about me. I guess the reason I came here was to find out if that was true or not true."

Ray's eyes got sort of big, and slowly a smile broke out on his face. I think I'd shocked him by being so forward. I know I'd shocked myself a little. "Is it true?" I said. "Or not?"

He just stared at me. Then after a moment he said, "Move over here."

"Did you say move over?"

"Yeah, move over."

I moved over. He reached out and put his arm around me and we both looked out his front window together. I lost my breath being so physically close to him—I guess most of my life I'd been wishing for this. "Why would I be crazy about a brat like you?" he said softly.

"I don't know. You don't have much sense."

"I don't, huh?"

I shook my head. "You might be a genius, but you don't have much sense."

"Oh, yeah?"

"Yeah."

"Well then, that must explain it." We just looked at one another, both grinning, and then our faces moved forward a little more—and before you knew it, we were kissing.

Well, I guess you can tell that this just about ends the story of how Ray Perkins and I finally got started.

MARY POPE OSBORNE is a first-rate storyteller and the author of over twenty works of fiction and nonfiction for all ages. Her books for young readers include *Run, Run As Fast as You Can*, the Magic Tree House series, and the Spider Kane mysteries, *Spider Kane and the Mystery Under the May-Apple* and *Spider Kane and the Mystery at Jumbo Nightcrawler's*.

Ms. Osborne and her husband, Will, divide their time between New York City and Bucks County, Pennsylvania.